Jimgrim, Moses, and Mrs. Aintree

Jimgrim, Moses, and Mrs. Aintree

Talbot Mundy

WILDSIDE PRESS

JIMGRIM, MOSES, AND MRS. AINTREE

First published in *Adventure,* volume XXXVI, number IV,
September 10, 1922,
"Moses & Mrs Aintree, copyright 1922 by Talbot Mundy,
copyright 1922 by The Ridgeway Company, Inc.

Jimgrim, Moses, and Mrs. Aintree

Chapter I

"We can reconstruct the whole of human history."

WELL, YOU KNOW how the firm of Grim, Ramsden, & Ross had its beginnings. We have had to use all our wits to save ourselves from being used by one government against another; rivals for political power have tried to employ us for their own ends and have succeeded more than once. You'd need the brains of an archangel and Satan combined to see through all the proposals that get brought to us. But there's reasonable money in it, and it's good fun; we've cracked a hard-boiled egg or two, and spilled some beans.

Strange gave Grim sole charge of the near-East end, purchased Narayan Singh's discharge from the army, and left the two of them in Cairo, planting Jeremy in London.

Strange and I went to the States, where, with the aid of his old office staff, we hammered through the organizing and incorporation; and while we were in the middle of all that, the first "view forward" came over the wires from Grim. Strange was in Washington.

MEET JOHN BRICE NEW YORK S. S. OLYMPIC. O.K. FOLLOW UP. GRIM.

I boarded the *Olympic* along with the pilot away outside Sandy Hook. It was early morning, but Brice was pacing the deck with a companion, and I observed them both for several minutes after a steward had told me who they were.

Brice was short, with a close-clipped gray beard, wiry, dried out, and resolute-looking. He stepped forward gamely with a decided limp, and made way for other people apparently uncon- sciously. I guessed his age between fifty and fifty-five.

His companion was about two inches taller, angular, and lean, a Scot whichever way you viewed him; a fellow with one of those noses that warn you not to waste persuasion on him, he'll decide for himself. He had heavy, sandy-colored eyebrows, broad shoulders, and a sort of side-swing that went with them. He wore a heather- colored Highland tam-o'-shanter and a small leather bag slung over his shoulder by a strap. The steward told me his name was Allison, and that he had shared Brice's stateroom on the voyage.

I introduced myself, and Brice chose one of those leather- upholstered corners in the smoking-room, and curled himself up cross-legged, staring at me frankly and fairly. He made no effort to disguise the fact that he was making an inventory of my pros and cons. His companion, seated next to him, did the same, perhaps not quite so sympathetically.

"We met Grim in Cairo," Brice began at last. "Allison and I are Egyptologists; we've been nineteen years in Egypt on behalf of the British Museum. The Egyptian law as regards antiquities is strict, and no kind of excavating is allowed without a permit, which is only granted to representatives of such institutions as the British Museum, the Metropolitan Museum of New York, and so on. All discoveries have to be reported, and nothing may be removed from the spot without permission in writing.

"Allison and I have specialized in the period during which the Israelites were in Egypt, with particular reference to Moses. Very little is known about Moses, historically speaking. In the biblical account not even the name is given of the Egyptian princess who is said to have discovered him among the reeds. It was our purpose, if possible, to throw light on all that period, establishing as many facts as might be —"

"And exploding a number of absur-r-d traditions," put in Allison. "We've disproved more than ye'd imagine possible."

"We have established the fact definitely that Moses did exist," Brice continued. "Whether or not one man wrote the *Decalogue*; whether or not one individual led that horde of Israelites and established the ten commandments and the law, we have proved that Moses did exist. He lived at a time that corresponds roughly with that of the Israelitish colony in Egypt. Our proofs, however, are missing."

"Do you expect to find them in New York?" I asked. "You'll find Moses' family is not extinct."

"Our quest has nothing to do with Jews," Brice answered. "The most astonishing thing about the Jewish race is their indifference to the monuments of their own past. Allison and I discovered a temple in which Moses undoubtedly studied that 'learning of the Egyptians' with which he is credited. There, we found the symbols and insignia that he used in the performance of the secret rites. Those have been stolen, and it might occur to you that Jews would be the logical people on whom suspicion should rest. But Jews have nothing whatever to do with it.

"We kept our discovery secret. It was so important, and the finds themselves were of such intrinsic value that it seemed wisest to close up everything until we could confer with the proper authorities regarding the disposal of what could be easily removed.

"ONE OF OUR staff was an Abyssinian, an individual named Gulad, who had been educated in America. He had served us faithfully for nine or ten years, and you know the proverb, 'If a comrade in arms is what you need, buy a Nubian slave; if you want to grow rich, buy an Abyssinian.' That fellow Gulad was the finest steward of resources that we ever had. Nothing escaped his notice. Nobody — not even a desert Bedouin — could steal from him, and he was sufficiently educated to appreciate the importance of antiquities, aside from the mere price they might bring in the open market.

"We had entered the temple through a hole in one corner of the wall after tunneling through sand for more than a hundred yards, shoring up the tunnel with timber as we went. Most of the important finds were in a great stone chest weighing several tons, almost the exact counterpart of the so-called sarcophagus in the King's Chamber in the Great Pyramid, only having a lid that fits tightly in place. The chest in the Great Pyramid has no lid.

"Whatever had been found outside the stone chest we placed inside it except for one small item. Then, with the aid of Gulad and ten men, we lifted the lid back, cemented up the breach we had made in the temple wall, pulled down about a dozen cross-pieces of timber from the roof of our tunnel, so as to let the sand fall in and close the passage against thieves, and came away, leaving Gulad on the spot in charge."

"You understand," put in Allison, "we never mistrusted Gulad for a minute."

"Never for a minute," Brice agreed. "He was as enthusiastic as ourselves. He used to sit and talk with us in the evenings, displaying an intricate knowledge of Bible history. He had theories of his own on a number of things that have puzzled antiquarians. He could read hieroglyphics. We used to give him worn and broken inscriptions to decipher, and he had a fair average of success with them."

"Aye, we were well taken in," said Allison. "We might ha' known it's not in the nature of an honest black man to be receiving letters from all quarters of the globe."

Brice laughed.

"It never occurred to us to ask what his voluminous correspondence was about. Now and then we'd see him writing until long after midnight in his tent by candle-light."

"We'd see his shadow on the side of the tent, ye understand," put in Allison. "We respected his privacy exactly as if he were a white man like ourselves."

"Well," Brice continued, "we left Gulad in charge, and took the train for Cairo. That meant a day on camel-back before we reached the railway, and a day and a night in the train. When we reached Cairo Galbraith, the official we had to see, was away; and we had to wait three days for him.

"When Galbraith returned — he arrived at midnight, and we kept him up all that night talking, though he was tired out — he thought our news so important that he made up his mind to return with us and have our find uncovered in his presence. That meant more delay. One way and another, it was eleven days after our departure before we arrived with Galbraith at sunset, tired and hungry on the scene of our excavations. The camp had completely disappeared! There did not remain one trace of it!"

"Nothing to eat! Nowhere to go!" said Allison.

"No lanterns or candles — nothing but a box or two of matches — no servants, except the two Arabs who had come with us to look after the camels we rode — no firearms — not a word of explanation. Nothing but Egyptian darkness, and the black mouth of a tunnel leading underground! We slept in the tunnel that night."

"Speak for yourself!" remarked Allison dryly.

"When morning came there was a little dim light down the tunnel, for it points due eastward, and for a short while the rising sun penetrates almost to the end. We saw then that the tunnel was not as we had left it. The overhead beams had been replaced, the loose sand carried out, and then three beams had been removed again to let sand once more block the tunnel. In other words, somebody had paid a visit to our find.

"It was three more days before we could get together another gang and dig through to our temple. The digging took another whole day, and then we saw that whoever had paid the visit in our absence hadn't taken the trouble to reset the masonry. The hole yawned as wide as if we'd never blocked it up, and nearly all the stones were pushed inside the building."

"I examined the cement at once," said Allison. "The masonry had been broken down before our backs were turned. That put outside conspir-racy out of the question. There was only one man who knew enough and had intelligence enough to dig straight to the spot and use crow-bars before the cement was dry. It was Gulad's doing."

"Be that as it may," said Brice, "we proceeded to examine the temple. It's a wonderful temple —"

"Per-r-fect!" exclaimed Allison. "The pattern and inspiration of the chastity of later Greek. design! But we'll not bore ye with technicalities. Proceed."

"Nothing in the main hall had been touched," said Brice. "We entered the smaller priests' chamber at the rear, in which we had discovered the great stone chest; and I told you how we had replaced the lid. That lid weighed a ton. It was set leaning against a wall. The stone chest was empty. Absolutely empty!"

"Man, ye'd have wept!" said Allison. "There were portraits done on gold of thirty-two initiates of the mystery, with their names inscribed; and beneath each portrait was writing of a kind never before unearthed in an Egyptian temple. Do ye know Sanskrit? Look at this. This is the single item we took with us that convinced Galbraith he'd better come back with us."

Allison undid his leather satchel and unwrapped from tissue paper a rectangular gold plate, about nine inches by six and more than a quarter of an inch in thickness. Its weight was prodigious. One side was entirely covered with writing etched into the soft metal. Allison laid that side downward on the table, and bade me consider the obverse.

"Don't touch! That's Moses!" he said, sitting back to enjoy the expression of my face.

THE GOLD HAD BEEN cut away smoothly to leave a portrait of a man in high relief. My previous mental picture of Moses had been taken from the cover of a school atlas. I imagined a man with whiskers like those of the man of Liskeard in the limerick, break-ing in his fury two stone tablets by the light of lightning, and kick-ing over a golden calf, while crowds of Israelites prostrated them-selves in terror before him.

The picture I had in mind of him was gigantic — six or seven times as big as other men — clothed in a thing like a purple bath-robe and with his toes sticking out from sandals that suggested seven-league boots.

This man had Jewish features subtly modified to pass Egyp-tian scrutiny. The beard was trimmed and curled like those of the statues of Pharaoh, and the headdress was the linen one of ancient Egypt, including the jeweled brow-band shaped like a snake.

Yet it hadn't been done by an Egyptian artist. You could easily recognize the touch of an Indian hand, betrayed by the skill with which the folds of cloth were handled and a kind of alive, compas-sionate humanity that the Egyptians never tried to picture — having none.

It was a face that you could stare at by the hour — attracting — fascinating — nothing repellent about it — amazing. It expressed not only humor, but the whole great cycle of the virtues, including wisdom. Not wisdom as the Egyptians represented it, static and cold. Wisdom that was so entirely wise that it could sympathize, and laugh with instead of at. I've never seen anywhere a face like that one, done in gold in Pharaoh's day.

"Can ye read Sanskrit?" demanded Allison. "That first line below the picture reads —

> Moses, son of Amram, an Initiate inducted to these Mysteries at the appointed time.

"The lines below that and on the reverse are the words of a hymn rather closely resembling the *Rig Veda*, but with significant changes that suggest parts of the first chapter of Genesis. It's conclusive proof that all known religion had its origin in India, as the Indians have always maintained. It proves that the man Moses was a living fact, and ergo that there's at least some truth in the legends attached to his name.

"Man!" he exclaimed excitedly. "D'ye realize that that San-skrit may be Moses' actual handwriting? That he may have done it himself with a sharp tool after the Indian whoever he was had finished the likeness! D'ye appreciate what that means? If we can get back the thirty-one others that Gulad the Abyssinian stole we can reconstruct the whole of human history!"

Well, there we were, steaming through the Narrows into New York harbor with a yellow quarantine flag at the masthead, staring at a portrait of Moses, who crossed the Red Sea without half as much mechanism to assist him and no steam at all. We were possibly handling a piece of gold that Moses actually touched.

"It's wonderful," I said. "I hope you succeed in catching Gulad and recovering the things he stole. But I don't believe this is a case that our firm would care to handle. You should try the regular detective agencies."

"Wait while we tell you the rest of it!" Brice answered. "It'll be hours yet before the port authorities let us land."

Chapter II

"MOSES MILES"

PASSENGERS began invading the smoking-room, but nobody interfered with us.

"It wasn't too late to preserve the temple," Brice resumed. "Galbraith sent for a police guard, after we had once more blocked up the entrance, and the three of us returned to Cairo to see what could be done."

"There are two ways of getting anywhere in Egypt — the railway and the Nile. They're both easy to police," said Allison. "If we had acted when we fir-r-st discovered the theft, the police might have —"

"I've had dealings with Gyppy policemen," I interrupted. "The size of the bribe is the only question. How did Grim get wind of this?"

"The heads of departments did their best," said Brice. "But all the subordinates are Gyppies, and the Gyppies haven't learned anything in forty years. The police didn't lose the trail, because they never as much as pretended to pick it up. They said it was a mystery, and shrugged their shoulders."

"And meanwhile," said Allison, "we had to submit to sar-r-castic r-remar-r-ks from men who never found more than imitation scarabs in second-century tombs, if ye know what that means."

"At last we had a talk with the High Commissioner," Brice resumed. "It was he who suggested our seeing Grim about it."

"Ye've a genius in that man Grim," said Allison. "We found Mr. Grim's quarters in Cairo occupied by a Sikh named Narayan

Singh, who said he was Grim's confidential assistant. He asked us for the story, and — you know how they bring you coffee in Egypt at the least excuse? Well, almost before I'd started a servant brought in coffee. He didn't seem to know any English; when I asked him in English for some cold water he didn't understand me. But instead of leaving the room after serving coffee the man squatted on the mat by the door and went into a sort of day-dream.

"When I'd finished telling the story to Narayan Singh, the servant collected the coffee cups and left the room. I asked if that was another of Grim's confidential assistants.

" 'Why, no,' the Sikh answered. 'That is Jimgrim sahib himself!'

"He came in presently in European clothes and apologized, explaining that we had caught him unawares, and that for the sake of practice he habitually stood and faced even little, unimportant emergencies. As he wisely remarked, big events are only little ones projected on a larger scale."

"Mon, the mon's a genius!" said Allison.

"Fortunately for us he knows the Near East like a book," Brice continued. "He analyzed what we had given him and boiled it down to the essential fad that Gulad is an Abyssinian, who was educated in the U.S.A. He found other Abyssinians in Cairo, and discovered that most of them regarded Gulad as a religious heretic, or backslider or something. Following that trail, Grim took a quick trip to Jerusalem, where there is an Abyssinian church. He was gone four days and returned with a light in his eye. Those Abyssinians had told Grim all they knew about him."

"That's the beauty of re*lee*gion," explained Allison. "Ye've always a thousand core*lee*gionists getting ready to expose ye at the proper time."

"Well, it seems that after Gulad's return from the United States he became a minor official of that Abyssinian church in Jerusalem. However, the seniors were jealous of him. He had studied Mormonism in the U.S.A., with particular reference to its success along business lines; and he pointed out that the colored people in the U.S.A. would prove a fertile field for propaganda of the sort he had in mind. But they turned him down; and the more he argued, of course, the more points he provided them on which to denounce him as a heretic."

"Ye see," explained Allison, "all novelty is heresy, new ways of getting rich included."

"At any rate, they turned him out of the church," said Brice, "and between that time and the day when he joined us he made various unsuccessful efforts to become a religious leader.

"Your friend Grim's reasoning was marvelous. He said to me that he considered one point obvious. 'If this fellow Gulad were a petty grafter, he would have stolen from you long ago. But he didn't steal. He has had charge of your petty cash for years, and actually saved you lots of money. If he were a petty grafter he might try to sell a goose that should lay golden eggs. Being a patient schemer, he'll set that goose to laying eggs instead. He'll play for power. You remember the plates of gold that the Mormons are said to have?' That was all Grim said to me for several days."

"But ye'll recall no doubt that I said things to ye," said Allison. "Ye'll remember my mentioning a per-r-fect catalogue o' new religious movements started by some chiel possessing a relic."

Brice ignored the interruption.

"Grim discovered in Jerusalem that Gulad's heresy, for which the Abyssinian elders excommunicated him, hinged on his interpretation of the law of Moses. That's important in the circumstances, Gulad has in his possession thirty-one gold plates covered with ancient writing, each of them bearing a portrait of a contemporary of Moses, and found in a temple in which Moses officiated. Even if he can't read Sanskrit, which is a practical certainty, he can show them to ignorant people and interpret them to suit his plans."

"And it becomes in consequence a verra reasonable theory," said Allison, "that Gulad entered our service because he knew we were sear-r-ching for evidence of Moses' actual existence. He persisted for about nine years. Ye can't restrain a measur-r-e of admir-r-ation for the r-rascal's deliber-r-ate per-r-tinacity."

"I still don't see where Grim, Ramsden, and Ross enter into it," I said.

"Grim saw at once. You'll see presently," said Brice. "Just listen. Grim pursued his inquiries day and night, not overlooking the important point that Gulad was educated in the U.S.A. He made another flying trip to Jerusalem, and this time I went with him.

"There was an American woman in Jerusalem, about whom nobody knew much. She was posing as a woman of wealth and making a clever display with what small private means she had. You know how a certain sort of enthusiast worships the very stones of Jerusalem? Well, she was that kind. But she seemed to want to own Jerusalem.

"Grim and I called on her after making a few inquiries. The U.S. consul knew more than he cared to tell, for in answer to Grim's questions he merely pursed his lips and shook his head. One or two Americans declared she was a rank impostor, but that was very likely personal pique. She was apparently more of a social climber than a politician. Impostor hardly seemed the right word.

"She was living in a pretty good house outside the city walls that she had coaxed from the Administration at a low rent. She had a way of worshiping a handsome British officer that some of them couldn't easily resist.

"Forty, I should say she is — forty-two — somewhere around that age. A big, handsome woman with unusual blue eyes and fine teeth. She had quite a household — four or five men and women from the States — nonentities, who did her bidding meekly.

They seemed to consider her almost as important as she thought herself, and it was from a very mild, hen-pecked-looking man of sixty that Grim learned an important point while we waited in the sitting room. She kept us waiting. She is the kind of person who does that.

"When she came down at last Grim had pumped the hen-pecked person dry, and after a few of the usual banalities about the weather and the Zionists Grim mentioned the name of a mutual acquaintance in Cairo. The personage being rather important she claimed to know him better than she really did, which suited Grim's purpose exactly. In that apparently purposeless way of his he touched on the subject of her home town somewhere in West Virginia and said untruthfully that the mutual acquaintance had told him that she was the leader of quite an important sect there. According to Grim, this mutual acquaintance had said that in West Virginia, Isobel Aintree was a name to conjure with. It was the hen-pecked person who had said that really.

"She was visibly disturbed, but walked straight into the trap. He had touched her vanity. She couldn't resist showing off. She had never mentioned this sect of hers to anybody in Jerusalem, but once she was under way Grim wouldn't let her stop. He pretended to find it the most interesting subject in the world, and under his fire of questions she admitted rather vaguely that her teaching was based on the Law of Moses.

"She came down finally under his persistent questioning to the bald fact that her sect has twenty-seven white adherents, and several hundred colored, none of whom were with her in Jerusalem. She said she felt that her mission in life was to benefit the colored people and she had hopes that the sect would grow. That brought up the subject of Gulad.

"She admitted that she knew Gulad. She had received correspondence from him. She had met him in Egypt on her way to Palestine. Grim pinned her down again by saying he knew Gulad intimately. He spoke rather as if Gulad were somebody whom only discerning people knew how to appreciate, and the rather subtle flattery of that proved too much for her discretion. She admitted that Gulad's correspondence had provided the main incentive for her journey to Jerusalem. She had hoped with his assistance to make Jerusalem headquarters of a sect that would some day include hundreds of thousands of colored people in all quarters of the world.

"There was nothing superficially vicious about that, of course. Scores of people have tried the same sort of thing, and a few have succeeded. Most of them go to the wall sooner or later. It looked like a single case of personal ambition masquerading as divine fire. But Grim asked her quite casually when she had seen Gulad last, and her whole character lay bare that instant.

"She wanted to lie, but that hen-pecked person was watching her as if pearls of price were pouring from her lips. She hesitated palpably, flushed red, tried to laugh it off, and floundered:

" 'Really, Mr. Grim, I'd rather not answer that question. I must ask you to excuse me.'

"From the look on his face you'd have thought Grim was shocked by the very idea of being inquisitive. She hinted it was time to go, but he sat still and flattered her a little more. That woman can eat up flattery like a furnace swallowing coal. He said that he should think she was the very woman to make something of Gulad.

" 'The fellow needs a guiding hand,' he told her. 'They say he has great plans. Do you know anything of them?'

"She flushed and refused to commit herself. Grim asked her how long she expected to remain in Jerusalem, and she answered that she felt her work in the holy city was about done; she might go at any time. Then we took our leave, and discovered that evening by asking questions all over the place that she was planning to leave for the States as soon as she could get passage.

"Still, we hadn't really connected her up with Gulad. We

merely had strong suspicions, amounting in Grim's case to intuition. We'd no ground on which to accuse her, and as Grim remarked, she was likely to be careful of herself.

" 'She's the kind of person,' he said, 'who likes to save the world by making her followers take chances. She's a kind of spiritual politician. If an idea works, it's hers; if it fails, it's the other fellow's, and she'll be the first to blame him.'

"A great student of character is your friend Grim. Everything turned out the way he said it would.

"We went up to Headquarters and dropped a hint that she might be intending to smuggle antiquities out of the country, and then Grim thought of another idea:

" 'Gulad,' he said, 'isn't likely to trust that plunder to an other's keeping. She's probably much too wise to risk being caught with the goods at present. If they're in "cahoots" (as he called it) there'll be some slick work done.'

"We went back to Egypt and searched the files of permits to travel and found to our astonishment that a passport had been issued to a man named Gulad, described as a French subject of Abyssinian origin, who had already left from Port Said by a steamer that called nowhere short of Boston. There was a warrant out; so we sent a cablegram and arranged to have Gulad arrested as soon as the ship reached port in about seventeen days' time. Now I'd have sat down and waited after that, but Grim didn't. He inserted a few lines in the newspaper, and sent a marked copy to Mrs. Isobel Aintree in Jerusalem. Also, he tipped off all the customs officials to keep a bright look-out, and arranged by telegraph to have word sent to us of all her plans. You see, we thought she'd have to engage passage and apply for a travel permit.

"But that woman is a wily one. She had obtained her permit two months before, available for six months, entitling her to travel in any direction she pleased. She sent a man down to book tickets on the train for Egypt, and we got word of that within two hours, over the Government wire. Then, if you please, she shipped the bulk of her luggage by freight to the United States, including nothing in it, of course, that was objectionable, and left northward for Syria in two motorcars with her household. Didn't use the train at all on British territory!

"The Arab government had fallen, and the French had not yet secured control; there were no officials at the border to hold her up. Once over the border she took train for Damascus, where the

French were only too glad to put her on the train for Beirut with every facility for leaving Syria at once.

"The motor-cars were hired ones. When they returned from over the border the news was out. There were two separate accounts, from two drivers, and copies of both were wired to Grim; checking them up he reached the conclusion that a colored man, described as her kavass, who traveled with the party, might be Gulad. He went to Jerusalem in a hurry for the third time, and decided that the fellow certainly was Gulad; so the plot began to clear decidedly. Gulad was in her house when we first called on her! Another man traveling in Gulad's name had shipped from Port Said to the United States with a French passport; and that's the point that baffled us.

"You see, the original warrant for Gulad's arrest had been issued over the French consul's signature. When we went to the consulate again to ask to have the French authorities in Beirut arrest that whole party, Gulad included, we found ourselves in check-mate. The man in charge was a typical bureaucrat, who asked whether there were two Gulads. A warrant had already been issued. Gulad was on his way to Boston, where he would be arrested by the United States police. No man could possibly be in Beirut and on the high seas simultaneously; and therefore he would not issue another warrant, because he did not propose to make himself absurd.

"Well, we tried to approach the French in Beirut more directly. But the cable was out of order. It is when international incidents are taking place. The overland wire by way of Palestine had been cut — by Bedouins, the French said; a coincidence that must have saved their censor a lot of trouble. The long and short of that was that Mrs. Aintree and her party, Gulad included, got clear away from Beirut. And in spite of all the ridiculous passport formalities at every frontier they contrived to cross Europe without our being able to learn which route they had taken until the information was too belated to be any use. So much for passports!

"We finally traced them to London, and Grim cabled to Jeremy Ross to pick the trail up there. He cabled back the same day to the effect that he had got in touch.

"Meanwhile," Brice continued, "Grim's assistant, the Sikh Narayan Singh, proceeded on the assumption that Gulad could not be wholly without intimates after nine years in Egypt."

"That was my idea," explained Allison. "It appealed to my

Jimgrim, Moses, and Mrs. Aintree

sense of the rid*ee*culous that any man should ignore the cir-r-cum-stance of Gulad having fr-r-equently received v*ee*sitors in camp; and the equally impor-r-tant cir-r-cumstance, that every one o' the v*ee*sitors was black. They used to spend days at a time in our camp. I was at some pains on more than one occasion to discover whether they were being enter-r-tained at our expense, and was gr-ratified as well as surpr-r-ized to ascertain that they paid their own footing.

"As long as he accounted in full for our stores and petty cash it was only reasonable to accord him the pr*ee*vileges due to any self-respecting man. Nevertheless, the unprecedented meticulousness of his honesty — in such a land as Egypt, mind ye, with Brice and me not scr-r-upling to feed our own guests from the expedition's stores — aroused my curiosity. So I discussed the matter with Narayan Singh, and he and I together ar-r-ived at certain definite conclusions. However, ye were speaking, Brice. Continue."

"Well," said Brice, "Narayan Singh discovered quite a little colony of U.S. darkies, more or less distributed in Alexandria, Port Said, and Cairo. Quite a number were sailors, who had deserted under your peculiar shipping law. Some were harder to account for on any theory of lawful activity, but they all seemed to eke out a living, and a few were prosperous. They were distinctly possessed of class-consciousness, mainly evidenced by insolence toward white men who chanced into contact with them.

"Among them were quite a number of the missionary-preacher type. Narayan Singh found at least a dozen who were living off the rest in fairly easy circumstances. Four or five seemed to be well educated, and at least one — a man named Moses Miles — had a bank account. I want you to notice that name Moses; it proved to be an important clue.

"We let Moses Miles carefully alone at first, and made a study of the others. It would not have been the slightest use for a white man to approach any of them. But their distrust and resentment, directed at all white men, apparently made them all the more inclined to accept the confidence of the Sikh. I don't pretend to explain it, but there's the fact. They seemed to despise the native African, to loathe the white man, and to regard the Indian as a possible friend.

"Narayan Singh discovered that Moses Miles was preaching a new brand of religion among those darkies. His name, it appears, was not originally Moses, but Horatio Augustus. He changed it when he adopted the new creed. The doctrine hinges on Mosaic law, and every initiate into its mysteries has to change his first name to Moses. Only initiates are allowed to preach. Other members are known as aspirants, and their chief duty seems to be to contribute handsomely to the support of the initiates. But there is an intricate ritual that —"

"Verra heathenish, abominable rites!" growled Allison, changing his position restlessly.

"— a ritual that is much too cleverly devised to have been worked out by Moses Miles, who possesses a dominant personality, and education of a kind, but no really high order of intelligence. Narayan Singh sought admission to the sect — People of Pisgah they call themselves. He failed, but he found out this: That these People of Pisgah through Moses Miles, were momentarily awaiting instructions from the United States, on receipt of which and accompanying funds four of their initiates and eight aspirants were to leave for South Africa and begin an intensive all-black campaign among the natives there — a campaign consisting of religion mixed with politics. And the interesting point is this: That the name of the great high-priestess whose orders they awaited is Isobel Aintree."

Chapter III

"A P.O.P. original charter member."

THAT LINER had a clean bill of health, but did not proceed to her pier. There began to be indignation meetings wherever there was room for twenty passengers to get together. But I noticed my friend Casey of the Federal Secret Service.

Casey regards the public as a herd of silly sheep with goats distributed among the herd at intervals. Regarded in the main, he doesn't love them; but I suspect that like a good sheep-dog he would grow old before his time and die of sheer disgust if deprived of his job. And wherever Casey strolls with both fists in his pockets and a look of bland indifference on his round, red face, you may safely bet there are human wolves or goats to be "fixed to rights" as he describes it.

After an hour or two he strolled into the smoking room and noticed me.

"Where are you from this time?" he demanded, sitting down beside us. "China? Borneo?"

I told him, and came back with the obvious question.

"Oh, nothing much," said Casey. "We got our man. We'd no picture of him and didn't know what name he'd travel under, but he's locked in his stateroom now with a bull to keep him company. We'll be alongside in about an hour. I hear ye've gone into the detective business with Meldrum Strange. Ye look like it! My boy, ye'll have to learn never to look interested. Unless they're clever men who're making trouble it's not interesting at all, and if they are clever ye can't afford to let 'em worry ye!"

"Judge for yourself," I answered. "This looks like a case for you, not me. You'll admit it's interesting and romantic."

"Then it certainly isn't for me! There's no romance in my business, Ramsden, my boy. I deal in card-indexes and photygraffs and thumb-prints. Romance looks pretty in the newspapers and the books o' Doctor Conan Doyle. But romance and crime don't mix, no more than the smell of onions mixes with ice-cream sodies. But I've an hour, and I'm willing to be amused. Which are ye going to do — talk elephants an' gold-mines, which I believe ye know about, or discuss this marvelous, romantic case with me like a hen discussing water with a duck?"

I preferred the farm-yard to the zoo, and made a start by introducing Brice and Allison.

"Now take his breath away," I said. "Produce the gold plate."

He studied it in silence for a minute.

"A picture of Moses, eh? I've seen Jews look like him. Take a stroll with me, and I'll point out to ye twenty or thirty men who might have sat for that picture. I suspect ye've man-handled the thing so that the thumb-prints are all overlaid. What's the writing all about? Some sort o' code? Have ye a key to it? It don't look to me like Yiddish."

Casey turned the plate over and over, holding it by the edges, for he regards thumb-prints as other men do first editions.

"Never mind," he went on. "Criminologically speaking, Moses is dead. How do ye propose to get this gold plate through the customs? Have ye declared it? Who's set a value on it?"

"We haven't declared it," Brice answered. "We have a permit authorizing us to take it out of Egypt in trust. Allison and I are personally responsible for it. Without this one we might find it difficult to identify absolutely the thirty-one others that were stolen, whereas with this —"

Casey whistled. He's a man of habit like the rest of us. The first bars of the last line of the chorus of a song that was beginning to grow whiskers in the war with Spain form his invariable, only war-cry —

"There'll be a hot time —"

"Have ye traced the thief over here? Ye'd better tell me all about it. Here, I'll slip it in me pocket, and ye'll have no trouble with the customs men. Which hotel? All right, I'll give it back to ye at the Waldorf this afternoon. I'll take good care of it. Now tell me all ye know."

Brice laughed; it might be a tall order to tell all he knew.

"Well," said Casey, "I understand ye've come after thirty-wan plates like this wan. 'Tis a big country, where there's room to hide such trifles."

"Trifles!" exploded Allison. "They're as impor-r-tant as Old Testament manuscripts."

"The Hell you say! Have ye any idee who took them. That might help."

Brice mentioned Gulad's name.

"Gulad? Gulad? Let me think a minute. There was a man named Gulad. Let me see. Yes, I remember. We held him in Boston. Colored man. The English would send from Aygypt for him. He'll be sent back to where he came from. Ye can arrest him over there in Aygypt."

"Who cares about him?" snorted Allison. "We believe that the real Gulad is over here, and that either he or a Mrs. Isobel Aintree has the plates."

"Aintree? Aintree? Isobel Aintree? Where have I heard that name?" said Casey. "Oh, yes. Go ahead; tell me some more."

His eyes had a harder, keener look.

"According to Mr. Ross, the representative in London of Grim, Ramsden, and Ross, she returned to the United States by way of London, bringing the real Gulad with her, and also presumably those gold plates," said Brice.

"But how did Gulad get into the States?" Casey demanded.

"It seems he's a citizen. Gulad applied for in London, and obtained an American passport. The witnesses who identified him were Isobel Aintree and two of her followers, who all swore to having known him for a number of years."

"Ah! It's easy when they've been naturalized," said Casey. "I haven't a doubt he landed safely, if he'd papers. Between you and me and that sideboard yonder, if the Lincoln Memorial in Washington D.C. was missing overnight, I'd suspect Mrs. Aintree as soon as any wan. She has a new religion, I believe, and wan's enough. Well, we're coming alongside. I'll say a word to the customs superintendent that'll save ye time."

HAVING SEEN BRICE and Allison to the hotel, I went to the office, where I found two letters on top of the morning pile, one from Grim and the other from Jeremy. Grim's was short and to the point.

> Confirming my wire, Brice and Allison are O.K. in all respects. Re theft, consult the federal police. Our interest

consists in unearthing a conspiracy to control the colored races of the world. Headquarters in U.S.A. Will report Egyptian developments as fast as they occur, and await instructions.

    JAMES SCHUYLER GRIM.

Jeremy's, on the other hand, ran to ten or eleven pages, and included a humorously accurate description of Brice and Allison. He wrote:

There's a sort of colored revival, combining religion and politics and using a secret religious ritual to bind all the darkies together. Mrs. Aintree is perhaps the head of it, and she and Gulad are as thick as thieves. She seems to have a hold on him or else he has on her, I hardly know which. I don't know what they have done with the stolen plates.

There is a dusky bishop here — he calls himself an "initi-ate" — who undoubtedly has seen them. Calls himself Moses Johnson. He is from Baltimore, and the name on his passport is Charles Abraham Ulysses Johnson. He is preaching — since be saw the Aintree woman — about the return of Moses to lead all African peoples into a promised land of their own; and he says that, whereas the law was written formerly on stone tablets, it is graven on gold plates now, together with portraits of the angels — thirty-one of them, he says; and he claims to know the name of every angel on the list. All the texts he uses in his sermons are from the Book of Exodus, and his favorite one seems to be the part about how the Israelites spoiled the Egyptians, looting all their gold and silver before they started for the promised land. Cable instructions.

    — JEREMY.

A little before three o'clock I called on Brice and Allison, who were discussing their prospects rather gloomily in a bedroom. Allison had made his mind up that my friend Casey was an impostor, who would melt down that gold plate and turn it into cash.

"In which case," he was saying as I entered the smoke-filled room, "you and I, Brice, are discr-r-edited and ruined men. Nor are we entitled to sympathy. We're simpletons."

Allison refused to be comforted by me. He had reached the stage of doubting everything and everybody.

"Mon, I know nothing at all about ye," he protested.

However, Casey came in presently, well pleased with himself, and laid the gold plate on the bed.

"I've a man I'd like ye to meet. Shall I bring him in?"

THERE appeared an undersized, wizened colored man, who stood in the door spinning a derby hat on one finger, eying us all nervously. He wasn't actually crippled, but produced the effect by shrugging himself up inside a blue serge suit a size or two too large for him. His white collar was about four sizes too big, and he had a thin neck like a tortoise's, all wrinkled horizontally as if he could lengthen or shorten it at will. What with gold-rimmed spectacles, white spats over brown shoes, and a big diamond ring, he was a strange enough apparition even for New York.

"You all wanted me?" he asked.

His voice was wistful. The expression of his mouth was somewhere between a smile and the beginning of a shout for help. He was bold, and yet fearful and suspicious, as one who has made up his mind to a course, but dreads the consequences.

"Come in. Stand there," said Casey, and the colored man obeyed. "Tell these gentlemen what your name is."

"They calls me Aloysius Jackson."

"Where are you from?" demanded Casey.

"Appleton, West Virginny."

"Live there all the time?"

"Mos' all the time."

"Belong to all the lodges in the place?"

"They ain't but one. I's soopreme, gran' —"

"Sure you are. How about religion, now? Member of any church in Appleton?"

"Sholy. The spirit o' man mus' be nutrified, Misto' Casey. I's a P.O.P. original charter member."

"What's P.O.P?"

"People o' Pisgah. Maybe you nevo heard. Folks has lots o' things they's ignorant about."

"Who runs that show?"

" 'Tain't no circus, Misto' Casey."

"We won't argue that. Who runs it?"

"It runs itse'f. De inspiration o' de Lo'd providin' tongues o' flame, it jes' nacherly spreads. We's not conscripted into limits. De P.O.P. —"

"Will pop, by thunder if you don't answer me! Who bosses the show? Who holds the money? Who gives orders?" Casey demanded.

"Missis Isobel Aintree is de Lo'd's appointed leader in this heah present dispensation, Misto' Casey. She's white folks."

Aloysius Jackson folded both hands in front of him and stood easy, apparently throwing one hip clear out of joint. It seemed that as far as he was concerned having "white folks" for a leader settled everything. Casey thought otherwise.

"Where is Mrs. Aintree?" he demanded.

"De Lo'd knows."

"So do you. In New York?"

Aloysius Jackson opened and shut his mouth, and his Adam's apple moved, but he said nothing.

"You've seen her this morning, haven't you?" said Casey.

"Misto' Casey, I's dumb. I's spiffically laid on not to make no mention o' the movements of de leader of de P.O.P. I claims privilege."

"All right," Casey answered. "Ever hear of jail? Ever been in Georgia?"

Aloysius Jackson's face underwent a subtle change of color and then set hard. Casey continued:

"Take a hold of yourself and think a minute! George Munroe, from Truckton, Georgia, won't go back for quite a while, unless his ghost walks. You recall him? President of the Indaypindent order o' Something-or-other wi' weekly cash benefits attached. Misused the mails, and razored the Federal officer who went to arrest him. That black man talked. He was a great talker. He died talking. You weren't his secretary now, by any chance?"

Aloysius Jackson seemed to prefer not to enter the ranks of great talkers. He swallowed his Adam's apple, regurgitated it, and made no comment.

"You weren't the secretary who couldn't be found to give evidence at the trial, I suppose. Another name, o' course in those days, but as likely as not the identical same fingerprints. Name of Alexander Hammond in those days, I think. That wasn't you?"

"Oh no, no, no, Misto' Casey. You're grievously mistooken. That wasn't me at all."

"Uh-huh! You're not on your trial — yet. Take care and don't commit yourself."

"I shoh won't, Misto' Casey!"

"It 'ud be easy to prove. You'd get ten years."

"Statute o' limitations, Misto' Casey! I provokes that statute. I provokes it consequentially."

"Invoke the Monroe doctrine, if you want to," answered Casey. "You don't know the law, my son. But, as I said, don't commit yourself. The Justice Department won't be bothered with you, unless you get rambunctious."

"Mr. Casey, sah, I's the least rambunctiousest nigger 'at you all know."

"Got pinched the other day, though?"

"Yes, sah, Misto' Casey, Ah got 'rested, but Ah'm not guilty; no, sir."

"Loaded bones, and liquor on the side?"

"True 'nuff."

"Possessing counterfeited money, too, I think?"

"Yes, Misto' Casey, sah, that was indicted against muh, but Ah's the victim o' conspiracy. Ah's the goat, sah."

"Out on two thousand dollars. Who bailed you? Mrs. Aintree?"

"Yes, sah, that lady took compassion on mah predicative."

"Why did she do that?" asked Casey.

"Isn't I a charter 'riginal member o' the P.O.P., an' aren't she leader?"

"That's a part of her duties, eh?"

"A part o' her prerogmative, Misto' Casey, sah. She's de Lo'd's anointed, an' she acts the part, sah, to perfection. She certainly do indeed."

"You've nothing against her, eh?"

"Against de Lo'd's anointed? No, sah, Misto' Casey."

"You'd not be scared to have all her doings known?"

"Ah convokes privilege. De fust rule of the P.O.P. is not to break de ninth commandment o' Moses by bearin' witness against her doings."

"Do you know anything about her that would make you afraid to report her doings?"

"Ah do, sah. Ah'd be plumb skeered to report her doings."

"Why?"

"Haven't Ah said 'at she's de Lo'd's anointed? Ah's not 'xac'ly anxious to be smitten, no, sah."

"So she's a smiter, eh? Then if she had some gold plates in her possession, and you happened to know it, you wouldn't admit it?"

"Ah admits nothin'. Posimetively nothin'. Ah'm dumb."

"Even in view of that case down in Georgia? Even in view of this charge of possessing counterfeited money? Even in view of the fact that you know I'm a Federal officer — and might — might I said — be able to get the case against you dropped — you're dumb, eh? Kind of a — fool, aren't you?"

"What you mean, Misto' Casey, sah, 'bout having the case against muh dropped? You mean Ah could go free?"

"If you're just a plain — ijjit," Casey answered, "you'll go to jail anyhow. Come on; what d'ye know."

"She's de Lo'd's anointed."

"Did she bring any gold plates back with her from Jerusalem?"

"Ah've not seen um, Misto' Casey, sah."

"You've heard about 'em, maybe?"

Aloysius Jackson swallowed his Adam's apple again, and looked miserable, but didn't answer.

"All right," said Casey. "Ever hear of a man named Gulad?"

"No, sir."

That answer was prompt and obviously truthful. You could see by the look of relief on the colored man's face that he was glad to be able to answer unguardedly at last. But Casey wasn't satisfied.

"She was in Jerusalem; you know that? How many people returned in her party?"

"Seven, sah. The sacred numbah, sah."

"Good. There were six when she left the States. Who is the seventh?"

"Misto' Moses."

"First or last name?"

"He ain't got but the one."

"Just plain Moses, eh?"

"Jes' Moses, sah."

"What sort of looking man is this plain Moses?" Casey demanded.

"Colored gel'man, sah."

"What else? Tall — short — fat — thin — medium — two legs or wan — ears or fingers missing — scars?"

"Medium, Misto' Casey, sah. Medium jes' about 'scribes him."

"What kind of medium? Goes off into a trance. Spiritualist? That sort o' medium?"

"Medium-size, sah. His spirit ain't medium. He's de leas' mediumest spirit ever was."

"You know him intimately?"

"No, sah. Ah's jes' heard him talk."

"What did he talk about?"

"Doctrine o' Moses, sah, an' spoilin' the 'Gyptians an' promised lan'."

"Where was that?"

"Colored folks promis' lan' in Africa, Misto' Casey, sah."

"I mean, where was it that you heard him talk?"

Aloysius Johnson closed his mouth tight and put both hands into his hip pockets.

"Ah don't 'xac'ly 'member, sah."

"Show him that gold plate," said Casey, turning suddenly to Allison; and Allison unwrapped it carefully.

"Ever see one like it?" Casey demanded.

"No, sah."

He was obviously lying. His eyes nearly popped out of his head, and he fidgeted nervously, shifting from foot to foot.

"You've seen a couple o' dozen or more of 'em recently, now haven't you?"

"No, sah."

"All right," said Casey, "that's as good as 'Yes.' "

He opened the door and whistled; a plain-clothes policeman appeared.

"Take him downstairs and keep an eye on him until you hear from me," he ordered; and Aloysius Jackson went out as he came in, walking like a cripple.

Chapter IV

"His name was Gulad."

THE DOOR had no sooner shut on Aloysius Jackson than Casey's air of optimism left him.

"Ye've a bad case," he said. "The plates weren't stolen from ye. They were taken from this old temple whiles y'r backs were turned, and maybe that's ag'in' the law of Agypt, but ye haven't proved that this man Gulad took them, nor what he did with them. If Mrs. Aintree has them how are ye going to prove that she didn't come by them legally? Possession, me boy, is nine points of the law. That colored man who came to Boston under the name o' Gulad will be sent back, for it's illegal to enter the country under a false name. But the real Gulad, who's a citizen, didn't change his name until after he got here; and he has a perfect right to call himself Moses or Murphy if he wants to, as long as his passport is O.K.

"Ye've got to prove first that the gold plates exist at all except in somebody's imagination. Then ye've got to prove that he has no right to them, and that you have the right to charge him with the theft. Then ye'll have to produce an extradition warrant, and on top o' that ye'll have to satisfy a judge that he's the identical man, and that there's evidence enough to justify his extradition. It don't look good to me. There's no law against importing bullion or antiquities. This isn't a case for me at all. I've nothing to do with romance, as I told me friend Ramsden this morning. But though the son-of-a-gun looks like an iliphant, Ramsden is really as romantic as a schoolgirl. It's a clear case for him and his new daytective company. Ye'd better hire Ramsden to look into the romantic end of it, and ye might make use of Aloysius Jackson to begin with."

"How?" demanded Brice and Allison together.

"Me friend Jeff Ramsden must consider that. It's my guess that if that black man is brought to trial the jury will acquit him. But I can throw a scare into him, and I will. I'll see him prisently, and send him up here for Ramsden to confabulate with. And now I'll have to be leavin' ye, for I've work to do. Me friend Jeff Ramsden knows how to get in touch with me at any time."

Brice and Allison sat looking at each other gloomily. They didn't recover, even when Aloysius Jackson came shambling in again.

But Aloysius Jackson was another who had not recovered. He was suffering from the Appleton, West Virginny, blues — sick at the stomach with dread of Terence Casey and the law, and of me in the bargain. When I shifted my bulk to answer the bedroom phone Aloysius Jackson jumped.

It was Casey at the phone.

"Y'r man's amenable," he advised. "Me and the bull downstairs had a session with him, and he'll eat out o' your hand from now forward. Keep him scared, and threaten him with me if he gets sassy."

Casey rang off, and I surveyed Aloysius Jackson for a minute. In addition to him I had to impress Brice and Allison, for a mistrustful client is bad, and two are worse — especially if one of the two is a normally suspicious Scotsman. I didn't feel nearly as confident as I may have looked.

I said, "do you want to die?"

"No, sah, Misto' Ramsden."

"Do you want to be all smashed up with this?"

I showed him a fist, and neither of mine is ornamental.

"Mr. Ramsden,'sah, Ah nevo done you no harm."

"You've got to do me some good."

"Ah's shoh willin'."

"Where does Mrs. Aintree stay?"

"'Partment seven, Roscoe House, Riverside Drive, sah."

"Where are the P.O.P. meetings held?"

"Fifty-ninth an' Ninth. Big top room, sah."

"How many entrances to the big top room?"

"Two, sah. Front way up f'r or'nary members. Rear way, back stairs f'r 'nitiates."

"When's the next meeting?"

" 'Morrow night, sah, nine o'clock."

"Any gallery in that big room?"

"Yessah. Back stairs go on up."

"You take me there tomorrow night," said I, "and if you don't hold your tongue you know what's coming to you."

"Misto Ramsden, sah, they search that air gallery f'r strangers. You-all is a stranger."

"You're the one who does the searching then," I answered. "No back talk! Your only chance of a whole skin is to do exactly as you're told."

"Yessah, Misto Ramsden."

"Meet me at my office tomorrow evening at six-thirty."

HE SLUNK OUT of the room looking utterly despondent. It was tough to have to go back on the "white folks" who had bailed him out of the Tombs. I've met colored men who wouldn't have done it, however scared they might be, for being afraid has nothing to do with being yellow. The test is, will you jettison your friends to save yourself, or to save them will you swallow your gruel — screaming or smiling — it doesn't really matter which? There is no other criterion. Aloysius Jackson was yellow.

That night I received *carte blanche* from Meldrum Strange who saw in a moment the international significance of Mrs. Aintree's doings. "She's playing for power. Some women take to that quicker than hop," he grunted. "Go after her hard. Spare no expense. Follow up without waiting to consult me, but keep me posted."

It was nine o'clock when I left him. I went straight from his hotel to Roscoe House on Riverside Drive to call on Mrs. Aintree; and I had the advantage of her, for she did not know me from Adam's off ox.

It wasn't exactly easy to get to see her, though, for her corps of followers had a system for keeping unwelcome visitors outside the door. They seemed to regard her as a she-pope, whom it would be sacrilege to intrude upon. However, the janitor downstairs regarded her otherwise. He said he intended to ask the agent to put her out, because all the other tenants were complaining.

"She rented the apartment furnished," he said. "Came alone, and. asked particularly whether the house was quiet. Didn't want dogs, children, or noisy house-parties. Looked good to me, and I fell. She moved in with five others, and they've been receiving colored people all day long ever since — one after another —

sometimes twos and threes. I've refused them the elevator; they've had to walk up, but they keep on coming. One comes half-a-dozen times a day. He's up there now if I'm not mistaken."

I was met at the apartment door by five of the inner-guard, and said that I brought news from Jerusalem for Mrs. Aintree's private ear. They were meek, but meekness is a much more difficult thing to deal with than audacity. They stuck to it that they were qualified to receive any message for Mrs. Aintree. They insisted that she was "not at home" to visitors, and might not be disturbed. However, I stumbled on the combination presently.

"My message is from Moses in Jerusalem," I said. "I'll tell it to nobody but Mrs. Aintree."

"How did you discover her address?" a mild man of sixty asked suspiciously.

"Moses of Jerusalem referred me to Moses of New York," said I, and they let me in.

"Is your name Moses?" they asked me. But I couldn't guess the right answer to that, so said nothing.

The room I was ushered into was just the place for a woman to sub-rent, whose means were nothing remarkable, and who wanted to make the utmost possible display. There was ten thousand dollars' worth of furniture in that one room — Louis the Lover stuff, all gilt and rosy cupids, with mirrors wherever there was room for one. You couldn't turn without seeing yourself reflected; and you could see whoever else was in the room from every possible angle by the simple process of selecting the right mirror.

Mrs. Aintree came in presently, and the meek fraternity retired — two men and two women, all going out through the same door without waiting to be told to; the fifth member of the household was in the kitchen, for I heard a clattering of dishes through the open door.

There was plenty of time to look at Mrs. Aintree, for she waited until the last of her team had left the room, and tried the door after them to make sure it was properly closed. I saw her from every viewpoint.

SHE WEIGHED considerably more than two hundred pounds, but carried the weight well. She would pass for a fine, big woman. A low-necked green and gold evening dress displayed her heavy shoulders, and exaggerated the forward tilt of her neck, producing an effect of great power; it was probably power of will, but there was somehow a suggestion of the washtub and physical strength won by leaning over it.

Her hair was carefully curled and dressed, a shade between brown and gold. She had a fine, bold forehead, that could wrinkle into angry vertical creases when she chose to be overbearing; and her big, full face was almost manly. She might have been a tomboy in her 'teens, and never have lost the yearning to compete with men.

But her most remarkable features were her eyes and mouth. The eyes were magnificent: large and brilliantly blue, looking frankly at you, not afraid to challenge, possessed of a certain humor, too, that seemed to boast of seeing through you and being on the whole amused. Her lips were perpetually parted, displaying fine white teeth a little too widely spaced. The two upper incisors touched her lower lip, and gave the key to her character — vampire will-power, drawing sustenance from living people. That woman had no use for dead ones.

I suspected her of considerable subtlety when put to it, but she chose to open on me with the crudest kind of hail-fellow-well-met stuff that ever a stock-salesman practised.

"Mr. Ramsden? So glad to meet you. I was a little disturbed by an unknown caller at this hour, but the first glance reassured me. We become psychologists, don't we, as we gain experience. I'd know you instantly for a man of calm and honorable purpose. I'm sure you've something tremendously interesting to talk about."

"I have," said I; and she looked hard at me.

Subtlety may be good, but I have none, and I hate it; don't want any.

"I've come to talk about your P.O.P. society," I said.

"Do you mean that you wish to join the P.O.P.?" she asked.

"I want to know about it. What is its basis?"

"The Mosaic Law."

"Is it a secret society?"

"No," she answered. "How can any universal law be a secret? But the Mosaic Law has always been misinterpreted. It was held to apply in the first place to the Israelites in Egypt, and to them only, but there is nothing universal about that. Every race, every people must eventually have its Moses who will lead them out of bondage; and everybody is a Moses who knows what Moses knew and acts as he did."

"Everything included?" I asked her.

"How is one to make exceptions?" she asked. "Who shall draw the line, and where?"

"Murder and spoiling the Egyptians are not objectionable?" I asked her.

"Killing isn't always murder," she retorted. "Nor is spoiling the Egyptians theft — if done in the right way. Moses said: 'Thou shalt not steal.' But he spoiled the Egyptians."

"And you are preaching that to ignorant people?" I asked her.

"Everyone is ignorant who doesn't understand the Law of Moses," she retorted. "My field, however, is among the colored races, who need their Moses as badly as ever the Israelites needed theirs."

"Have you thought of the consequences?" I asked. "If they interpret literally your teaching that killing is not murder, spoiling isn't theft, can you imagine what might take place in the United States, for instance?"

"What happened to the Egyptians?" she answered. "Tyranny entrenched has no rights that anybody need respect. If people insist on suppressing the colored races, they must take the consequences, just as the Egyptians did. If the British insist on suppressing the colored races within their borders, they must also take the consequences. The same applies to the French, the Portuguese, the Spaniards, the Brazilians, the Italians — to every people that is holding colored races in subjection."

"And why should you be the Moses for the colored races?" I asked. "You're not colored."

"No," she said. "Neither was Moses an Israelite. Whoever understands the law of Moses becomes a Moses. I accept no responsibility. I teach. I do not make laws, but teach the law that was propounded on Sinai centuries ago."

"Why do you call your sect the P.O.P?" I asked.

"People of Pisgah? It was from Pisgah that Moses saw the Promised Land. My followers rise to Pisgah heights and see what lies before them. They become prophets, in a degree that depends on individual inspiration and zeal."

"Do they perform miracles?" I asked, casting about for questions that might tempt her to keep on talking.

"They become able to accomplish their purposes in ways that unenlightened people can not understand. I will give you an instance: Just as the Israelites were given laws engraved on stone tablets, and the Mormons have writing on gold, we needed a standard by which to test our authority and our actions. Well; you are familiar with the Bible, Mr. Ramsden? You recollect how patient Moses was? How he went into the wilderness for forty years —"

"Yes," I said; "he murdered an Egyptian and ran away into hiding."

"He found what he needed in the wilderness," she answered severely. "An initiate of ours did the same thing. He, too, went into the wilderness — the same Egyptian wilderness. In considerably less than forty years he was led to find exactly what was needed — the law engraved on gold by the very hand of the original Moses himself!"

"I'd like to see that," I suggested.

"Mr. Ramsden, that is presumption. Among the Israelites none was allowed to enter the Holy of Holies. You must attain to the level of high-priesthood before it would be even safe to show you what our initiate found. That initiate of ours was led to find the gold plates through great self-abnegation and sincerity; and none can get the right to see what he found, in any other way."

"Was his name Gulad?" I asked her, and she looked startled, but recovered instantly.

"Yes," she said; "his name was Gulad."

"Mameluke Gulad?"

"Yes. But he has taken the name of Moses. That is the prerogative, and in fact the duty of all initiates."

"I'd like to see him," I said. "Is he in New York?"

She paused a long time before answering that. Finally she lied by innuendo.

"No," she said, "you can't possibly see him at present."

"The janitor told me that he is in your apartment now."

"That janitor!" She smiled, but looked hideously angry — then fell back on flattery.

"Mr. Ramsden," she said at last, "I told you that those who understand the Law of Moses attain to more than the usual measure of discernment. It is clear to me that you are no ordinary man. Whether you are destined to be one of us or not, I do not know, but I feel impelled to grant your request. Honesty is a key that opens doors."

SHE PRESSED an electric button, and the door was opened by the meek man of sixty, who smiled like a verger viewing a bishop, at close quarters. She tossed him her order, and in another minute in came Gulad, the meek individual closing the door behind him silently.

"Moses, this is Mr. Ramsden. He has expressed a strong desire to see you."

Gulad-Moses looked irritated. He was black of countenance, with quite a lot of yellow in the whites of his brown eyes. Patient I dare say; cynical certainly. Dressed in black evening clothes, with a fair-sized diamond in his shirt-front. An upstanding, lithe figure, as are many Abyssinians, but with the unmistakable Abyssinian head that doesn't provoke confidence, whichever angle you view it from.

Moses-Gulad looked at me, failed to make me feel uncomfortable, recognized my suspicion of him, and made no effort to seem friendly.

"Why do you wish to see me?" he demanded.

He stood with that sort of sneer on his handsome lips that can be turned into a smile on the instant if necessary — standing deliberately close in order to compel me to look up at him, which is a trick understood by most bullies. It was mighty tempting to send him staggering back on his heels.

"I came to see those gold plates you brought from the Near East," I answered.

"Who told you anything about them?"

If you've never heard an Abyssinian trying to take the upper hand of a white man you don't know insolence. Mrs. Aintree looked positively scared, and something that may have been tact, or may have been just foolishness, impelled me to save the situation for her.

"A gentleman named Brice described them to me," I answered.

Gulad-Moses began to betray nervousness, but covered it pretty well.

"Mr. Brice will have to be arrested if he tries to interfere with me!" he retorted. "Brice heard of my discovery, and has been trying ever since to get possession of the plates on all sorts of pretexts. He and Allison are nuisances — two crooks — who don't yet realize what kind of man they have to deal with! Tell them from me that I've stood all the nonsense I'm going to."

"I'm not a public messenger," said I. "I'm interested in those gold plates."

He laughed cynically, and turned his back. But the mirrors served my purpose as well as his. Instead of his catching the expression of my face off-guard as he intended, he betrayed his own. It was malignant, alert, cunning, and combined with a dislike of me and a suddenly born distrust of Mrs. Aintree — or so I read it. He threw one swift look sidewise at her that should have made her blood run cold if she had seen it. Then, facing suddenly about again, he sneered:

"I suppose you are one of those newspaper people? Tell your newspaper that for a million dollars they may see the box in which the plates are kept, and that is all!"

"Really, Mr. Ramsden, they can't be shown to any except initiates," Mrs. Aintree explained, in an effort to calm the atmosphere.

Gulad-Moses was beginning to pace the floor and work himself into a passion.

"Already too many have seen them!" the black man snarled, pausing in front of her. "Too many fools have seen them! I warned you. I warned you. I warned you! I told you what would happen if you talked! A man is a fool to trust a woman! You admitted to this person that you had seen the plates — you fool!"

She bit her lip. Before she could answer him he turned on me.

"I don't care for your newspapers! Tell your newspaper, and tell Brice and Allison that I laugh at them. The police shall arrest Brice and Allison if they annoy me. I am an American. I have a lawyer who will protect my interests. Brice and Allison are liars and crooks, and that is all I have to say!"

At that he stalked out of the room and slammed the door.

"You must excuse him," said Mrs. Aintree. "Possession of those plates and the responsibility have wrought on his nerves. He is hardly himself. He is normally the very essence of politeness. But even Moses of the Exodus, you know, used to fly into a rage at times. We who have spiritual vision, Mr. Ramsden, have more to bear than other people, and should be excused if at times our tempers get the better of us. Is he right in assuming that you represent a newspaper?"

"No," I said. "Brice and Allison interested me, that's all."

"I suppose that is the Mr. Brice who called on me in Jerusalem along with a Mr. Grim. I wondered at the time what their real object was. Gulad tells me they have been persecuting him for years. He says that Brice managed to steal the most important of the plates. Did Mr. Brice confess to you that he has one of the plates in his possession?"

"I'm not Mr. Brice's confessor," I answered. "You haven't told me yet about your plans."

"You mean the agenda of the P.O.P? We have none in the usual meaning of the word. We will bring light to the colored races and let the light do its own work. When you take two and multiply by two, you don't choose the result; it becomes four automatically. When we teach what we know to people who are as yet in darkness, the result is equally logical and takes care of itself. It is our business to sow the seed. The growth is sure to upset human calculations."

"I've heard anarchists make statements similar to that," I said.

"Ah! Anarchists. Well, they have the courage of conviction, hut no knowledge. We have both. Moreover, we have authority in writing done thousands of years ago by the man who gave the ten commandments to the Israelites."

"Then you mean to upset the world, if you can?" I asked her.

"Do you deceive yourself that the world is worth leaving as it is?" she retorted.

"My impression is that you and your friends are planning wholesale murder, anarchy, rape, ruin, and misery simply for sake of the power it may bring you personally."

"Strange!" she said. "My intuition told me you are capable of understanding — even of being one of us. But we sometimes make mistakes. You've nothing to do with the police? Well, Mr. Ramsden, let me give you some advice. For your own sake let this matter drop! Don't try to interfere with us! You would find yourself up against a knowledge — a power — a force that you are incapable of understanding. You will be ground to powder! And now I have important work to do, and must bid you good evening."

We shook hands, and I laughed and went. But she did not laugh. In the mirrors I could see her scowling at my back.

Chapter U

"Oh you Promis' Lan'!"

GREAT MEN and women have great vision but can keep their two feet on the ground. Frogs who would be oxen let their vision carry them away into realms of sheer absurdity, where all sense of proportion vanishes.

I don't doubt Mrs. Aintree had tremendous vision. I don't doubt she thought she was entirely right. She fondly imagined Gulad was a man of destiny sent to help her by the Powers that Be, whereas he was an obvious character, using her for his own purposes. The worst of it is that the visionaries seem able to do more harm in twenty minutes than the other fellows can accomplish good in twenty years.

I had seen and heard enough to convince me that Mrs. Aintree was contemplating not much less than revolution under the thin veneer of religion.

So I pulled Meldrum Strange out of bed at his hotel and thrashed the problem out with him from the beginning. Finally we sent for Brice and Allison at midnight, and they agreed to place the whole investigation in our hands; but Allison was so anxious over his loss of the plates that he made me the strangest proposal I ever listened to.

"Man," he said, "ye'll be honest as long as it pays deevidends, I haven't a doubt of it. I'm a poor man, but I'll mak' it profitable for ye to be honest. In the course o' cir-r-cumstances, if ye've any skill in following clues, the r-rascals who've stolen those plates away will be offering ye money to corrupt ye — more by a verra great deal than I could pay ye. But I take it ye're a reasonable man. Ye talk like one who has a fair pride. Ye'll keep a fair bar-r-gain. So if ye'll turn down any offer o' cor-r-uption, I'll give ye the half o' my savings, just to encourage ye. Ye shall have an auditor's cer-r-tificate, and the half of all I've got! It isn't much, I'm warning ye, but honest money will feel better in y'r pur-r-se than a lar-r-ger sum gotten by standing in wi' Gulad and his like."

I hardly knew whether to laugh or swear at him, and ended by doing both. He would have been far more satisfied if I had agreed to take his money. The next thing the dour old faithful did was to hire another detective agency to keep an eye on me. Their man came to me perfectly frankly that afternoon, and to save trouble I promised to write out a daily report of my doings and mail it to his firm!

WHEN EVENING CAME, and Aloysius Jackson put in his appearance, I took a taxi to the corner of Fifty-ninth and Ninth, where Aloysius pointed out a narrow door in a red brick, building less than half a block away. There were stores on either side of the front entrance, but the four upper stories were all shuttered and there was nothing to show what use was made of them, except for the three letters P.O.P. done roughly in white paint on the left-hand side of the dim hallway, where one cobwebby light burned overhead. But the wooden stair-treads showed the marks of countless heavy feet, and the recently varnished handrail was already beginning to show fresh signs of wear.

I made Aloysius go up first, and followed him, as a precaution against surprise, but there was nobody up there yet. The echo of our footsteps died away as we rested at last in front of a door, on which some former employees of a tailoring concern had scrawled their opinion of the boss together with an alleged portrait of the gentleman.

"That air gallery is inside here, Misto' Ramsden, sah. Got no key, sah."

He felt less afraid of me at the moment than of the dusky. brethren who might call him to account for admitting me. "You all might bus' that ole door in," he suggested, trembling.

"Open her up," I said, "or —"

A look at my fist convinced him. He pulled out his clasp-knife, inserted the big blade cleverly, forced back the catch, and stood aside to let me pass through on to a narrow gallery that extended the whole length of one end of a room about sixty feet by thirty. The walls were white-washed, the windows shuttered, and the only light came down from a dusty factory skylight that reflected the glare from an electric advertisement on a neighboring roof. The floor of the room below was arranged to seat about a hundred people on inexpensive folding chairs, and at the end opposite to the gallery was a small platform covered with red carpet, against which, along one side, stood a piano that had decidedly seen better days.

There was a pile of reserve chairs stacked against the gallery railing near one end; so I spread those out a little, cautioned Aloysius Jackson, and shut myself in. The only entertainment during the hour that followed was provided by a rat, whom curiosity devoured, but who stubbornly refused to make friends because I had no food to offer him except tobacco.

Then came the sound of voices, footsteps on the stairs below, a snatch of song, and the jingle of keys, followed by Aloysius Jackson opening the door to search the gallery for strangers. The lights in the hall were switched on suddenly, and the fear on Jackson's face was something to marvel at. He shut the door behind him, walked the length of the gallery noisily to call attention to the fact that he was doing his duty, cautioned me with a finger raised to his lips, and let himself out again, slamming the door with a noise like a thunderclap. A minute later I heard him reporting to somebody below that the gallery was empty.

The hall began to fill rapidly with colored men, and one of them went to the piano, beginning to play all the latest ragtime airs with that peculiar careless ease that no white man ever seems able to imitate successfully. Some of them pushed chairs out of the way and began to dance, and when a dozen colored women entered, the place was in an uproar for several minutes. It was about as little like a religious meeting as a bicycle resembles Camembert cheese.

The initiates began to arrive after a while, and sat on the platform in a row with their backs against the wall, all dressed alike in well-tailored black suits. Aloysius Jackson, who seemed to be acting janitor for the day, shuffled about arranging chairs, glancing up in my direction every now and then. Through the interstices of the stacked-up chairs I counted nine initiates, running the gamut of shades between black and ivory. They were a self-satisfied, well-fed, smug-looking lot.

THE RAGTIME CONTINUED almost until the moment when Mrs. Aintree walked up the aisle in evening dress with orchids on her bosom, followed by Gulad-Moses. Then the tune changed, and everybody stood up, bursting into song —

> *"If* there's a devil, and it's true, true, true,
> *Who'd* rob the devil of his due, due, due —?"

It stopped when she reached the platform. There she stood facing them with one hand raised, her back to the initiates, and Gulad stood half a pace behind her. The utter silence in which the congregation waited for her to speak was fair evidence of her hold over them. They didn't even shift their feet or glance about. You could hear the long gasp as one or another grew tired of holding his breath.

"Friends," she began after a full minute, and then paused. She knew the full value of keeping them waiting. "I am glad to see so many of you here this evening. Has the gallery been searched?"

From the back of the hall Aloysius Jackson answered that it had been, his voice quavering.

"Who is that?" she demanded. "You, Aloysius? You searched? Very well. I want to emphasize the need of always doing that. We can not be too careful. Anyone might lurk up there and overhear things that must not be made public for the present."

No general commanding ever addressed his staff with more aplomb than she displayed. Her voice rang with emphasis, and her attitude was one of absolute command.

"We will have only one hymn tonight," she went on, "and we will leave that for the end of the meeting. There have been complaints about the noise we make, and the sooner we get our own hall, where we can follow inspiration without restraint, the better. Let there be more whole-heartedness! Let me see you give more generously — fewer dimes and quarters, and many more dollar bills! Show by your generosity in giving to our cause — that your claim to be entitled to self-determination is not nonsense, as your critics say it is. Let the key-note of your loyalty be Give — Give more — Give magnificently!"

I did not dare move to look around, but it struck me that her speech was falling flat. The initiates behind her, who presumably drew salaries to pay for their fine clothes, beamed approval, but I heard no murmur from the congregation signifying eagerness to pour cash into the coffers. She sensed the backwardness, for she changed her tone.

"Why am I your leader? Because in no other way can you enter your promised land and come into your God-given rights. Remember the Children of Israel. Before they were able to spoil the Egyptians they had to obey their leader and give all their gold and silver to the common fund. It was after they had done that, not before, that their leader showed them how to appropriate the wealth of their taskmasters and then led them through the wilderness into a land flowing with milk and honey."

That suited them better. There began to be a little restlessness. Talk about plunder just over the skyline was more agreeable than demands for cash down.

"Perhaps you are bewildered,"she went on. "Perhaps your courage fails when you think of the power of the people who oppress you, who grow richer every day from your starved and unappreciated efforts. But the children of Israel labored under the whip to make bricks without straw, and they broke the yoke! How? By concerted effort in obedience to their divinely chosen leader! Remember that we have the precise instructions of that identical leader engraved on gold, and buried away in the sands of Egypt until at the appointed time your new Moses rediscovered them!"

At that reference to himself Gulad did not actually pat himself on the back, or make any specific gesture; nor did he smile broadly, or say anything; but he came out of a mood of meditative discontent into the broad sunshine of complacency like a butterfly emerging from a chrysalis, and I could almost feel his self-esteem physically from where I crouched.

"Perhaps you feel discouraged by the thought that all your promised land is occupied by alien peoples," Mrs. Aintree went on. "I answer you: Remember the children of Israel. They were four hundred years in bondage. It was often their fate, as yours has been, to be carried away into captivity. But they returned, laden with the spoils of their captors."

They applauded that part of her speech, clapping and stamping their feet, the noise increasing until one big buck in the middle of the hall bawled out:

"Oh you promis' lan'! Oh you li'l land o' milk an' honey! We's on our way!"

She held her hand up, and silence fell as if she had touched the button that controlled them.

"It may seem an insuperable obstacle to you," she continued, "that that vast continent of Africa — your native land — your birthright — is all staked out by European powers, whose trespass is upheld by armed men and artillery. But remember again the children of Israel! They marched into a land that also was occupied by trespassing nations whose military power was considered overwhelming in that day. And what happened? The Lord fought for the children of Israel, and the trespassers were put to the sword and driven out in confusion. The Lord will fight for you, if you obey your leader and respect this new Moses."

THE NEW MOSES preened himself again, but she did not step aside to let him make a speech, and I began to get the hang of the situation. There was rivalry between her and Gulad. He had the gold plates. She had the congregation and the gift of speech. They had tried to combine in partnership, but were as jealous of each other as a pair of rival politicians. I think it crossed his mind to step forward and begin to say something, but she forestalled him with a contralto voice that rang down the hall magnificently.

"You are known as the People of Pisgah. Why? Because you have vision. Because you can rise to the heights of inspiration and discern the destiny in store for you — destiny that depends on strict obedience! You are more fortunate than the children of Israel — for many reasons — in many ways."

"Oh you promis' lan'! You promis' lan'! You milk an' honey, we is on our way!"

"You have their example. You have the record of mistakes they made. You can judge how they failed and suffered when they disobeyed. But when they were utterly obedient how they surged on to one success after another, becoming possessed, because they were obedient, of all the wealth of their enemies! On those terms, will you obey or not?"

That got them. The hall broke into tumult. They were willing to promise anything on terms of *quid pro quo,* and their enthusiasm broke bounds until she once more raised her hand. This time she had more difficulty in getting them to be quiet, and it was two or three minutes before she could make her voice heard. Then she struck the vein of promises again.

"You are more fortunate than the children of Israel! They had a land of milk and honey to go to, but it was a little land with limitations, surrounded on every side by enemies. You have a whole vast continent surrounded by the sea! The sea that surrounds Africa will protect you! They had a waterless desert to traverse, and it took them forty years. For you there is only a friendly sea that can be crossed in fourteen days, or less! They had to enter a land that was full from end to end of enemies. For you there waits a continent, where millions Of your own race will receive you with open arms — with tumults of rejoicing! They will make common cause with you to drive the tyrants from your coasts."

That set pandemonium loose. Some of them began singing. I caught fragments of three different hymns from opposite ends of the room, and one bull throat drowned out all the others, roaring —

"Oh, you've got to be a lover of the Lord, of the Lord,
If you want to go to heaven when you die —"

The man at the piano struck a chord, and in a moment they were on their feet; but she stilled them with a gesture of magnificent command. A weaker woman, a less clever one in her own way, would have let them shout themselves hoarse and sing themselves into hysteria. But she chose to show authority and check them in the same sort of way that a skillful driver controls his horses after giving them their heads for half-a-minute. There was lightning in her eyes and regal power in her gesture. They grew still.

"You are more fortunate than the children of Israel! They walked. They had to content themselves with such trifles as were considered wealth in those days. They drew on the resources of Egypt in a hurry, taking what could be obtained to balance their account with the Egyptians, who were poverty-stricken compared with your oppressors. You are in no hurry! You have the wealth of a continent to draw on, such as neither Babylon or Rome could show in their palmiest days. Is obedience a too great price to pay for that advantage?"

Then came the gist of her address — the rhubarb in the sugar-coated pill — the point that made Gulad blink and swallow, taking all the gilt off the ginger-snap of being the new Moses.

"Obey me," she thundered, "and your continent — your promised land — is yours!"

Obey her, not Gulad.

WELL, THEY PROMISED HER. They rose like one man to their feet and filled that hall with a din surpassing the dust-laden tumult of political conventions. It was no wonder that complaints had been received about the noise. The pianist cut loose like one man playing a duet, but made no impression on the din; I could see his hands moving and his figure swaying, but heard no note of the music; and the dry dust rising off the floor and swaying in clouds about the hanging electric lights made me cough until the tears came. But I was perfectly safe up there; they were much too excited to hear me.

It must have been fifteen minutes before order was restored. There were individuals who had to be forcibly suppressed. One man upset half-a-dozen chairs and danced until their occupants fell on him and forced him to the floor, where he lay under the lot screaming with idiotic laughter. And through it all Mrs. Aintree stood smiling patronizingly, every now and then turning to say a word to Gulad, who sulked and said nothing. When more or less silence fell at last I thought she was going to bring Gulad forward and let him say something; but not a bit of it.

"It does my heart good," she said, "to see you so enthusiastic in a righteous cause — so enjoying your clear vision of success. But don't forget that from your Pisgah height you see the promised land without the miles that lie between. There are difficulties to be overcome that lie in wait for you, difficulties not surmountable except by patience and persistence. We need courage, pertinacity, and secrecy combined. Courage that will throw off tyranny. Pertinacity that shall not flinch or falter when your tyrants bring about delay in order to keep you a while longer in thrall to them. Secrecy that shall confound the enemy by keeping him in the dark as to our plans. Dare all things! Persevere in the face of delay! Say nothing! Tell nobody! These are my injunctions to you."

She paused to let another outburst of enthusiasm have a full two minutes' lease before continuing with the self-satisfaction of the demagogue who feels the crowd helpless under hand.

"And why this secrecy? Are we afraid? Not we! But if you warn the Egyptians in advance your chance will be gone. We have work to do before we make our exodus. Our missionaries must go out to Africa and prepare our friends yonder for what is coming. We must raise funds. We must teach. Our propaganda must extend to the towns and hamlets, not only of New York and West Virginia, but of all the United States, and Canada and South America as well!

"Most of you are destined to be missionaries. As porters, as hotel servants, as laborers — in all the menial capacities to which your tyrants have reduced you — you will go forth and sow the seed, working whenever opportunity presents itself. And since every laborer is worthy of his hire, your expenses will be paid from the contributions to our cause that you yourselves take up. The half of every dollar that you take, you keep; the other half you forward to headquarters, where it will be used to swell the general fund. There will be no auditing; no check on you. We People of Pisgah must learn to trust one another before we can expect to have an empire at our feet."

That sentiment. struck home! Neither South Sea Bubble nor Blue Sky Mining stock ever looked better to investors than that proposal to share and share alike in all the voluntary contributions without audit. The few faces that I could see took on an expression of hopeful avarice that would have passed muster in the zoo at mealtime, and the initiates on the row of chairs at the rear of the platform beamed almost drunkenly.

"And now," she said, "we have made almost noise enough in this neighborhood for one night. It is our usual course to conclude these meetings with prayer suitable to the occasion; but there is a stipulation in the lease that we must be out of this hall by ten o'clock, and I shall have to trust you to say your prayers at home on this occasion.

"We will conclude our meeting with your favorite hymn that I wrote specially for you, and that I think most of you know by heart. During the course of the hymn our initiates will pass among you and take up a collection, and at the conclusion I will ask you to pass out of the hall quietly and disperse, calling as little attention to yourselves as possible."

The man at the piano struck up. They rose to their feet excitedly, and burst into the song I had heard earlier in the evening:

> *"If there's a devil, and it's true, true, true,*
> *Who'd rob the devil of his due, due, due?*
> *In the dark the devil's lurking,*
> *For our downfall ever working,*
> *But we'll laugh to see his finish in his own bad brew!*
>
> *Let the devil wear the shackles that he forged — so — well!*
> *Ours shall be the kernel, his the empty shell!*
> *For the Lord the earth is ridding*
> *Of the fools who did his bidding,*
> *And they'll tumble with the devil into Hell — Hell — Hell!"*

I didn't stay to hear any more, but took my chance of opening the gallery door unseen and slipping out. Nevertheless I was seen from the platform, or at any rate the door was seen to move. Four big black men came out of the door below and intercepted me, demanding insolently what I wanted.

"Is this where the K. of P. meetings are held?" I asked.

"Cain't yo' read?" demanded one of them. "Don't it say P.O.P. down thah on that wall?"

"What was you doin'?" asked another one, crowding me close. He may have got his muscle heaving coal, and he seemed rather to relish the prospect of a scuffle with a white man. It's fortunate that colored men have good thick skulls, or there would have been a case for the coroner. One made the gross mistake of getting between me and the stairs to bar my way, and as his jaw was thrust out quarrelsomely I hit that first. He went over backwards and crashed downstairs on his head and shoulders before the other three could razor in, and I took the stairway at a running jump, landing on my victim as I passed, taking out of him any wind that might have remained, and surely delaying pursuit because he lay across the stairs and they had to feel their way over him in semidarkness.

Once outside there was no further danger. Men whom Meldrum Strange had sent came on the run the minute I showed myself. They were most of them colored men, who had worked for banks and suchlike institutions, but two were white.

I ordered the colored men to shadow the initiates; The white men's job was to watch Mrs. Aintree and her accomplice Gulad, not interfering with them but instantly reporting the first sign of any contemplated move.

Then I phoned Meldrum Strange and set off in a hurry to find Terence Casey, for I wanted his advice. But hurry did not help me much. That boast of his that I would know where to get in touch with him at any time was easy to say off-handedly but not demonstrable. I chased him from pillar to post, by phone, messenger, taxicab, and on foot, being sent on from one place to another by secret-service men, every one of whom had seen him that evening because he had been the rounds and given them instructions for what they said was an important case.

And I found him at last near midnight, in a little back room over a place that had once been a saloon, pulling off his socks preparatory to getting into bed with his shirt and trousers on. There was a telephone beside the bed, and I guess he used that place habitually.

"Well?" he said smiling, as an old woman ushered me into the room. "How's the new case coming? Have ye cut y'r eye-teeth yet?"

"I told you it was a case for the police," I answered, "and it is."

"Sit ye down on the bed, Ramsden me boy, and unburden the sorrows av y'r soul. Tell me all about it."

I repeated to him word for word all that I could remember of Mrs. Aintree's speech, and added my own comments.

"Damn," said Casey, when I had finished. "Go home and sleep, unless ye want to share this bed with me. That's nothing! Ye should have heard the devils talk in Butte around the mining camps. She's just a hot-air expert out for exercise and small change. You go home to bed, me boy, and dream about y'r fee ye'll get from Brice and Allison!"

Chapter VI

"No form of abstinence. No fasts. No saints' days."

MELDRUM STRANGE tried to interest the Attorney General's department, but without success. Terence Casey's secret report on the subject was a deciding factor. He denied to me having sent in any such report, but with a smile in his eye.

"Ye're like all amatchoor daytectives, Ramsden, me boy. Ye think that y'r case is a lallapolooser, and all the departments are banded together wi' red tape to keep ye from savin' the body politic. Ye've been reading Sherlock Holmes — good reading too; I don't blame ye. But I'm busy. Go an' 'tend to y'r case an' don't worry me. When ye're weary of such foolishness; go back to huntin' iliphints — a game ye understand."

But we don't have to be guided by political considerations or by the barometric state of someone's bile in Washington, D.C. We put our whole force on the problem, regardless of expense. Jeremy wrote from London that two white missionaries and a number of colored ones were actively preaching similar doctrines to Mrs. Aintree's in the London slums and other places where the floating colored population could be found. And Grim wrote from Egypt to much the same effect, adding that the story of the gold plates had spread southward into the Sudan and was causing the Administration no small concern. Moses being regarded as a mighty prophet by Christian and Mohammedan alike, the colored missionaries were finding no difficulty in spreading their new doctrine, which found readier acceptance because it included the expulsion of all the white races from Africa forever. Grim wrote:

The thing looks bad, and is growing worse. The

natives are getting cockier than ever and less inclined to reason. The story of those gold plates has gone to their heads. They're beginning to talk already about reversing the position and subjecting the white races to their dark authority.

The mystery is where all the money comes from to finance these missionaries. None of them do any work. I've traced a small part of their funds to random subscriptions taken up locally, but there seems to be a central fund that baffles discovery. The money being spent out here greatly exceeds the receipts from donations, so it's obvious someone is paying the piper. These missionaries out here live like fighting cocks, and are growing arrogant.

One thing that makes their propaganda easy is that they preach no form of abstinence. No fasts. No saints' days. No Ramadan with its forty days of thirst and hunger. The conventional moralities are all scoffed at. A man according to their doctrine may have as many wives as he can support, or can be induced to support him. They object to too much prayer, and teach that a man's instincts are his own best guide. You can imagine how such a doctrine as that will draw adherents from all quarters.

There's someone in authority. When a missionary gets orders to go elsewhere, he goes, and another takes his place. They teach absolutely strict obedience, and keep the source of the orders a mystery; but there's a man who calls himself Moses who gets cables in code from New York. I've managed to get copies of some of the cables, but can't puzzle out the code because I can't discover what book the numbers refer to.

This is all too ably thought out and organized to be the work of Mrs. Aintree. That woman is only half-clever. I believe you will find that there's some much abler man or woman behind her, who uses her for a stalking horse to hide his or her own identity. Whoever it is certainly displays a knowledge of the native races far beyond the ordinary as well as an understanding of crowd-psychology in general.

If you examine Mrs. Aintree's antecedents you may discover from whom she got her ideas. They're distinctly second-hand. And my advice is the same old stuff I was always rubbing into you when we hunted together in Arab country. Get close. Be patient. Stay on the job until you force a showdown. Appear to give the enemy a free hand and "Stop, Look, Listen!" Watch out you don't get murdered. Mrs. Aintree, I think, would draw the line at murder personally, but not impersonally. I know her sort; they preach, and some fanatic does the killing, as happened in the case of Lincoln and McKinley and lots of others I could mention.

Above all, don't be discouraged by official cold water and what may look like official impediments placed in your way. Don't talk, or consult authorities. Root right in until you've found the individual who's really running things, and then go for him bald-headed. Yours for peace without perquisites.

— GRIM.

As a matter of fact we had already followed in most respects the line Grim recommended. For instance, we had looked up Mrs. Aintree's past, and nothing could afford better proof of Grim's almost uncanny judgment than the result of our inquiries. She had been connected with a School of Esoteric Thought conducted in Boston, Massachusetts, by an East Indian named Pananda, whose teachings had had considerable vogue until Mrs. Aintree, who seems to have been his favorite pupil, led a revolt against him and tried to set up a school of her own in opposition.

I MADE A TRIP to Boston and called on this man Pananda. He was living in style in a house in the Fenway, had a Chinese butler, and kept me waiting in an extravagantly furnished anteroom for three quarters of an hour as if he were an up-to-date physician with a fashionable practice. I might have been more impressed by his importance if there had been anybody else on the waiting list, or if I hadn't been curious enough to look about me. There was a peculiar arrangement of mirrors in the room that brought to mind the somewhat similar arrangement in Mrs. Aintree's apartment, so I sat still and examined them, going about it as carefully as if I knew I were being watched.

Mirrors are mighty puzzling things, unless you are accustomed to manipulating them. If you don't believe that, just arrange a piece of paper so that you can see it in a mirror, and without looking at the paper, but observing its reflection in the glass, try to draw a square and then to cross the square with diagonal lines. It was quite a long time before I had figured out that those mirrors were so arranged that a person looking into one of them from one angle would get a full view of anyone who happened to be in the room.

It wasn't so difficult after that to discover that the point from which the view was to be had was in the middle of the wall above where I was sitting, so that I had my back to the view-point and face toward the light. I chose another chair and examined that wall. There were two mirrors, draped with magnificent eastern hangings, and between them a thing shaped like a Persian shield, only instead of being solid it was pierced to form an intricate pattern. Anyone could see easily through its interstices, provided there were a corresponding hole in the wall behind it, but he would have to be standing on a support of some kind, because the lower edge of the shield was more than six feet from the floor. I returned to the first chair and set my foot on it, with the idea of examining the shield more closely, and it was exactly at that instant that the Chinese butler opened the door to announce that Swami Pananda would see me. He saw my foot on the chair, hut made no comment.

I was ushered into a large, square room, hung like the first with Eastern draperies but containing very little other furniture. A magnificent carpet covered the entire floor, and at one end of the room were a short couch and an armchair made of teak.

Against the wall on my left, at a point that corresponded with the Persian shield in the anteroom was a gilded image of the Buddha, an enormous thing more than eight feet high, and the large plate-glass windows opposite suffused it with light, making it the one outstanding object in the room. The whole effect was sumptuous, yet magnificently simple and produced a far from disagreeable impression.

Pananda was seated on the couch, and rose to meet me. He was a rather fat man but not flabby, dressed in semi-Indian clothes of yellow silk — a sort of comfortable compromise between the easiness of India and Western notions about decorum. He wore yellow silk socks and yellow, soft, morocco-leather slippers, but no jewelry whatever. For the rest, he was a mild-looking person with remarkable brown eyes, a rather bulging, broad forehead half-concealed under a yellow silk turban, and a smile that was winning, to say the least of it.

"Welcome, Mr. Ramsden. Pray take that easy chair. So you came to talk to me, but I shall do most of the talking, if you permit. You saw through my little device for analyzing visitors; my Chinese butler interrupted your investigation; it's part of his business to keep an eye on strangers. You'd be interested, I dare say, to see how the arrangement works; the head of the Buddha swings outward on a hinge — look!"

He got off the couch and showed me, pressing a very simple

swing catch behind the Buddha's ear. The whole head swung forward like the leaf of a door, disclosing the rear of the Persian shield through a small hole in the wall.

"You see? By standing on the Buddha's lap I can observe anyone in the next room from every angle. I often have a lot of quiet amusement, watching visitors unknown to themselves. The longer I keep them waiting, the more completely they give themselves away as a general rule. Then they come in here and tell me silly little lies about themselves and other people. I introduce themselves to themselves for the first time usually. They go away astonished. Sometimes I charge them a big fee, sometimes not, depending on the circumstances. I shall not charge you anything, for instance."

"I had no intention of paying you a fee," I answered.

"I know you hadn't. You came here to investigate me. My brother, you're a very easy man to read; rather honest, but not nearly as honest as you think you are; a hunter — you have done a lot of killing in your time; a resolute man, and a very faithful friend — those are your two strong points; not quarrelsome, but combative — too willing to settle any argument by strength and brute force. You are one of the strongest men physically, and even in some ways mentally, whom I have met in recent years. As for your present purpose — you came to talk to me about Mrs. Aintree. Am I right?"

"How did you know that?" I demanded.

"Oh, that's very simple. I notice you're not a policeman; you have none of the earmarks of the hired investigator, and I confess that puzzled me for a while. But I put two and two together, you know; that's my business, and I'm an old hand at it. Look at this."

I READ THE WORDS "Isobel Aintree" in a bold, thick handwriting at the foot of a letter that he pulled out of his pocket.

"Isobel Aintree is disturbed," he explained. "She's beginning to be sorry that she left my fold — I give lessons, you know. She called me on long-distance, and I went to see her in that apartment she has leased in New York. She wanted advice. Ha-ha! They all come back to their teacher in the end! She told me something of her great plans, and begged me to tell her how to manage an individual named Gulad, who seems to be giving her a lot of trouble. I interviewed this Gulad, and he was very angry with her for having summoned me. He accused her of talking too much, and gave me to understand that she had been especially indiscreet toward a man whose name he didn't mention, but who he said came to see her one evening. That man was obviously yourself!"

He eyed me humorously as if he expected me to see the connection and enjoy the joke. But I didn't.

"I recognized you at once," he said. "She learned that arrangement of mirrors in a room from me. When you sat down in my anteroom I noticed that you recognized the same arrangement. I had quite a little fun observing how long you took to puzzle out the sequence of reflections from mirror to mirror. Gulad had described to me an individual fairly well answering your description. I have in my pocket a letter from Mrs. Aintree, in which she complains that some agency in no way connected with the police is — to use her eloquent description — camping on her trail. She states that all her former friends have been cross-questioned, and her whole past has been inquired into, and begs me to answer no questions in case that anyone should apply to me. When my butler brought your card I added all that together, and the total amounted to Mr. Jeff Ramsden here to ask questions about Mrs. Aintree. Not very clever, was I, after all?"

"Do you intend to answer my questions?" I asked him.

"Certainly. Why not? And now you are wondering just how much credence you can place in my answers. Hah! My friend, if you had studied people as scientifically as I have, you would never wonder at my being able to read your thought in that way. Your emotions flit over your face one after another like the pictures on a screen, Mr. Ramsden. Well, as your expression suggested a moment ago, I am something of a mountebank, it is true, but a rather more than usually honest one. I used to be an altruist, as I thought, pure and simple, but have awakened since to consciousness of a vein of absurdity underlying all my efforts to improve the human race.

"My diligent and more promising pupils mostly deserted me in a half-taught condition, as Mrs. Aintree did, for instance, and set up in opposition, sometimes even going so far as to denounce me as an impostor. The stupid pupils simply wouldn't learn, and what they did learn often disagreed with them. So I have been gradually discontinuing to teach, and devote myself nowadays more to giving advice to folk in difficulties, sometimes for a fee, and sometimes gratuitously. I make the rich ones pay, believe me! To that extent I am a mountebank. I frequently charge for performing tricks as simple as the one I played on you just now. On the other hand, I believe I do no harm in the world, and I know I have frequently done good."

"No harm in the world?" I retorted. "You admit that you taught that Aintree woman, and then turned her loose to —"

"Pardon me, my friend, I did not turn her loose. She left me in peculiarly irritating circumstances, and not only set up an opposition class of her own but told lies about me. She accused me of immoralities and I don't know what else. However, I bear no malice. Malice, my friend, poisons whoever entertains it rather than the one against whom it is supposedly directed, and one of the first lessons I teach is the absurdity of harboring malice.

"When she sent for me the other day I went at once. And I gave her some very good advice. It was so good, and so disagreeable, that she did not offer to pay my expenses to New York and back — not that I would have accepted the money; but she did not know that I would not accept. One of my first principles is never to accept money from anyone whom I have not helped or am unable to help. There is no helping her in her present mood; she is headed toward disaster."

"You might save a lot of trouble for other people," I suggested, "by helping to speed her disaster before she involves too many in it."

"I would hardly do that," he answered. "Good does not come out of evil, although the opposite argument looks plausible at times. The confidences of my pupils, or of people in distress who come to me for advice, are absolutely sacred. It must be obvious that I could not conduct my activities on any other basis. I would go to prison before I would violate a confidence. But a pupil who is disloyal, and who uses my teachings corruptly, as Mrs. Aintree, for instance, does, forfeits in a degree the right to be treated in that manner; in a degree, please understand me, only in a degree."

"You said you would answer my questions about her."

"I did. But my answers will depend upon the questions. I did not tell you in what way I will answer them. Suppose you try me with a sample question to begin with."

"Very well," I said. "Who is coaching Mrs. Aintree? It isn't Gulad, for he's a rather ordinary smart-Aleck; and the scope is much too vast for any woman of her caliber. Who is directing her from behind the scenes?"

"Shrewd!" he remarked. "Much too shrewd for you, in fact,

my friend! Obviously she is not the only one who receives coaching! Someone else suggested that question to you. Am I right?"

"Yes. But who is coaching Mrs. Aintree?"

"IT IS no breach of confidence to answer that," he said meditatively. "Bhopal Gosh — a Hindu — more or less a countryman of mine."

"A teacher like you?"

"Not at all like me; but a teacher nevertheless. He has also been known as 'The True Mahatma,' 'The Golden Guru,' 'The Buddha Redivivus' — and by some of his American reporter critics as 'The Perfect Piece of Cheese.' He has other self conferred titles, too many to remember. I believe that in his heart, to himself in private, he candidly admits that he is the wisest man on earth. He once had the effrontery to make to me proposals that were laughable. I am not ambitious, unless to bring a little comfort into a distressed world, and I gave him what I believe was very good advice — in this room; he was sitting in that armchair. My advice enraged him. He is an immensely powerful man physically. I should say he is even more muscular than you are. He has a temper like a typhoon. I had my work cut out, to escape from the interview uninjured, and before he left he swore to make me sorry I had ever met him.

"Well, Mr. Ramsden, I am not given to regretting experiences. They are the chief part of our education. But I knew that that man would destroy me if he could. It was for me to prove that he could not destroy me. He commenced a campaign against me by propaganda, which was less difficult to deal with than if it had been more subtle. At that time he, too, was conducting classes in Boston, charging prodigious fees and appealing in the main to women, which made it rather easy for him to approach my women-pupils indirectly and win some of them away from me.

"Mrs. Aintree was the first to go, and she took several others, five of whom are still with her. She has subjected those five to her arrogant will, by making believe to possess inspired knowledge that is really far beyond her present power of attainment. She is a great play-actor. I made the mistake of teaching her too much psychology before her character was ready to digest such dangerous knowledge; and Bhopal Gosh, who is a man without any conscience but with a rare ability, proceeded to cram her foolish head with much more of the same sort; so that she has become a creature who is clever and foolish by fits and starts.

"She mistrusts Bhopal Gosh, because no one can have intimate dealings with him without discovering his crude dishonesty of purpose; but she respects his knowledge and his adroitness, to use the least objectionable word that seems applicable. And she is certainly afraid of him. He has taken good care that she shall be afraid of him. That is his invariable method. He has excited her ambition and fed it; and now he makes her believe that with one stroke of the wand, so to speak, he can throw her in the discard and deprive her of all chance to attain the influence over people that she yearns for."

"Why should she come to you for advice, if she thinks so highly of Bhopal Gosh?" I asked.

"Because he has left her in New York with rather more responsibility than she can manage. Mere ambition, Mr. Ramsden, doesn't confer ability. She has what Freud might call the emperor-complex. She seeks to dominate, and knows enough to take the first steps toward her goal. But the first steps are the easiest and the most deceptive; they lead to a stage of bewilderment, which she has reached. And in that peculiar stage of mind she sent for me to give her good advice, having so far lost her sense of right and wrong under Bhopal Gosh's tuition that she actually believed I would help her to consummate his evil purposes in his absence. She said that as my former pupil she was entitled to advice from me. Well, so she is. I gave her some; but she is very far from taking it."

"Where has Bhopal Gosh gone,?" I asked him.

"That might be difficult to discover. He is one of those crafty individuals who expects his victims to tell him all their secrets as a point of good faith between pupil and teacher, but who keeps his own counsel perfectly. He makes his preparations a long while ahead. The mere fact that he has started on a journey, let us say westward, is no proof that the East is not his real objective. He has made a tremendous amount of money, because some of his pupils have been successful in business, and it has been easy for him to get inside knowledge of stock exchange transactions. One of his pupils, who afterwards went to prison, was in the confidence of one of the largest brokers in Boston. So he is able to pay for what he can not obtain in other ways."

"Do you suppose he has gone abroad?"

"Possibly. He started for West Virginia, where this P.O.P. society of Mrs. Aintree's had its beginnings. If he has gone abroad from there he probably applied for his passport and booked his steamer passage months ago."

I stared at Pananda for more than a minute.

"And now you are wondering," he said, "whether it is jealousy of Bhopal Gosh that makes me talk of him in this way, and just how far my information may be trusted. I hardly blame you. Every human being is dishonest — with himself, if not with other people; when we overcome dishonesty we shall cease to be humans and become something better. But I am doing my best for you, and that is very likely better than you could get elsewhere on the particular subject of which we are talking. I am not jealous of Bhopal Gosh. It would annoy him intensely to know that I pity him, yet that is the fact. However, I pity a great deal more the unfortunates who have been inveigled under his control. You may believe implicitly every word I have told you about him."

"I dare say you could tell me a great deal more?" I suggested.

"Possibly. I could tell you a great deal more about some of his victims, if that were permissible. But you see my position. I am already half a charlatan, because I descend to such tricks as that hole in the wall behind the Buddha's head. I would be wholly a charlatan if I betrayed confidences made to me in good faith. The truth of the whole matter is that I am a lazy man, extremely willing and, in many cases, able to give comfort to others, but fond of my own comforts also. You would like me to enter the lists with you against Bhopal Gosh and Mrs. Aintree. That thought has been hovering across your mind for several minutes. I shall disappoint you, I'm afraid."

"I've got work out of lazier men than you," I answered.

"I don't doubt it. But you see, they weren't clever men. You can't get work out of a clever man who doesn't wish to work. I am rather clever, and besides, I have no wish to avenge myself on Bhopal Gosh. Revenge is too costly altogether, and not worth while."

"Aren't you interested in protecting Bhopal Gosh's victims?" I demanded. "He and this Aintree woman are planning to throw the world into the devil of a mess."

"My interest lies only in helping those who actually come to me for help," he answered. "You came to me. I have tried to help you. But my gifts are limited. I can give you advice, but not material assistance."

"Have you heard anything about some stolen gold plates?" I demanded.

"Oh yes. Mrs. Aintree told me all about them. If you wish me to talk of them you must tell me everything that you know about them first. Then I shall be able to determine how much I can say to you without infraction of others' confidences."

So I told him, beginning with Brice's story and ending with an account of the meeting at "Fifty-ninth and Ninth," New York.

"Very interesting," Pananda exclaimed at last. "Most deeply interesting. There is very little that I can add to your information, but I can give you some good advice. Those plates are, comparatively speaking, harmless in the hands of the Abyssinian Gulad or of Mrs. Aintree, because they both lack the necessary brains to use them to the full advantage. But in the hands of Bhopal Gosh — they would be worse than poison gas and dynamite combined! If you can prevent his getting them, you will be rendering the world a service. Bhopal Gosh is possessed of devilish ingenuity. He knows perfectly well how to excite men's passions by an appeal to their religious instincts or their superstition. Those plates would better be destroyed than in the hands of Bhopal Gosh."

"What is he? Crazy for power?"

"He has power! He is mischievous. Go after Bhopal Gosh but take care for yourself; for he is more dangerous than all the other dangerous men you have ever met, all put together!"

Chapter UII

"Murdered at seven fifteen."

I LEFT PANANDA'S HOUSE with mixed feelings, but on the whole felt inclined to trust his information. The difficulty to my mind was to believe that here in the United States one man — and he a foreigner — could have the gall to plan the world-wide outrage that was apparently intended.

Nevertheless, by the time I reached New York next morning I was inclined to believe, in spite of what I have seen in various quarters of the world in the way of lightning-like adoption of a new idea by widely scattered colored races, that the whole thing was a mare's nest; that the gold plate incident was a simple case of theft; that the P.O.P. was a harmless organization that might keep out of mischief otherwise possibly turbulent individuals; and that Mrs. Aintree was a simply ambitious crank, who would melt presently in the heat of her own hot air.

But Meldrum Strange, who was waiting for me in the office, stolidly chewing one of his dark cigars, threw another light on things. He showed me the collected and typed-out reports of our men in the field. They were from all over the United States, and described secret meetings of the P.O.P., followed by local strikes, violence, and trouble on a small scale generally. There had been a particularly bad local outbreak at Appleton, West Virginia.

"And this is the latest," he said, passing me a longhand report from one of our New York men. "It was too late to get into the morning papers."

He looked delighted. He was in his element, sitting there in the middle of the net like a strong, good-natured spider, feeling the threads of events vibrate to his touch. Along with his deliberate altruism there is a schoolboy passion for intrigue. It was rapidly coming to the point where a murder to him produced the same sort of effect that news of a necessary operation does on a young surgeon. He was almost audibly chuckling. And murder it was, according to our man's account.

> *Mameluke Gulad was murdered at 7.15 this morning in his room at Riley's Hotel on Ninth Avenue by an unknown colored man, who entered through the fire-escape. Nothing in the bedroom was disturbed, but Gulad's jaw was nearly wrenched off by the assailant, who gagged him and then stabbed with a broad-bladed knife. No knife was found, but the wound under the ribs on the left side is several inches long. Death must have been nearly instantaneous. The police have charge of the body.*

"Our man phoned in at 8.30," said Strange. "I happened to be down here early, and the first thing I did was to phone to Mrs. Aintree and tell her all about it. She'll be round here before long, unless I'm much mistaken."

I began to tell him about Pananda and Bhopal Gosh, but his surmise was accurate enough. Mrs. Aintree sent her card in before I was half-through, and the two of us received her in Strange's private office.

She was dressed up to kill, in a lavender creation, with a hat that would have looked too youthful on a maiden of seventeen, and breezed into the office with that sort of unsolicited familiarity that annoys you by its insincerity. She marched on Strange with her hand held out:

"Are you Mr. Ross? Mr. Ramsden I know already, and I met Mr. Grim in Palestine."

"My name is Strange," he answered, bowing slightly.

"Strange? Are you the gentleman who telephoned to say that Gulad has been killed? Pardon me, but how like the pictures of General Grant you look!"

"Be seated, madam, and tell me what you want," he answered.

"Are you connected with the police in any way?" she asked, trying to ignore his brusqueness.

"No, ma'am."

"What is this firm? There is no description on the door or in the telephone book."

"We do an international business."

"How did you learn about Gulad's death?" she asked.

"One of our men was passing the place, and saw the assassin escape."

"Well?" she said. "You know something about Gulad or you wouldn't have telephoned to me at once."

"Gulad stole thirty-one ancient gold plates from an Egyptian temple, and brought them to this country with your connivance," Strange answered. "Where are the gold plates, Mrs. Aintree?"

She hesitated, and Strange took a long shot — took it deliberately, as if he were firing at a mark.

"You may stand accused of having that man murdered for the possession of those gold plates," he said. "This firm has been commissioned to recover those plates for their lawful owners. If you know where they are you'd better say so."

"I don't know where they are," she answered. "The pity of it is, I don't know."

She wrung her hands and seemed inclined to cry.

"Gulad would trust nobody with them. He lived in that little back bedroom in Riley's. Hotel — a very third-rate place with all kinds of undesirable characters frequenting it constantly, and we begged him to be careful with them and not leave them in his room."

"Who besides yourself was sufficiently interested to caution him?" Strange interrupted.

She hesitated palpably; again. It was my turn to take a long shot.

"Was his name Bhopal Gosh?" I asked.

"How did you know?" she demanded.

"Continue, ma'am," said Strange. "What happened to the plates?"

"I don't know. I wish I did. If I knew where to lay my hands on them I would dispute their ownership with anyone! I've consulted a lawyer. We were quite within our legal rights in keeping them; but now I don't know what to do. You've no notion how much depends on the possession of those plates! Who has commissioned you? Why don't you take the commission from me instead? I'll pay you anything in reason to get them back. If you find them and hand them over to anybody else you'll be robbing me — us."

"What do you think Gulad did with them?" asked Strange. "There was nothing in his bedroom when the corpse was found.

The man who escaped was carrying no package. You must have some idea. What might Gulad have done with them? Did he rent a strong-box?"

"I don't know. He had a little money, and opened a bank account at the up-town branch of the Cotton and Woollen National Bank. I went there on my way here, and they wouldn't tell me anything."

I SIGNALED STRANGE and walked out, leaving the two of them talking. A taxi took me to the Cotton and Woollen National, in less than five minutes, and I was admitted at once into the manager's office.

"Does a man named Gulad rent a strong-box here?" I asked. "He has been murdered. You'd better seal the box up."

He took me down into the strong-room, and showed me an entry in the day-book. The box had been opened and its contents removed that morning, exactly three minutes after nine o'clock. A colored man, apparently a negro and giving his name as Simon Borrow, had arrived with a letter signed by Gulad authorizing him to open the strong-box. As a photograph of Simon Borrow together with his signature was attached to the letter the bank had had no alternative. Borrow had gone away five minutes later in the same taxi that brought him, leaving the strong-box empty. The bank detective had fortunately noted down the taxi's number, and of course the bank had kept the letter and photograph.

I studied the picture of Simon Borrow carefully, and was far from being convinced of his negro origin. He looked more like a native of Bengal. it was the picture of a heavy man in the prime of life, with massive shoulders, an enormously thick neck, and a big, round head, broad forehead, heavy jaw, a rather pug nose, and a smile of supreme self-satisfaction. His eyes were large, heavy-lidded, and cunning, and there was a scar underneath the right one. The individual features were strong and not ill-proportioned. Taken together they depicted an immeasurable guile, contempt of other people's intelligence, and ruthlessness.

The strong-room clerk told me that the man's physical strength was prodigious. He had put the contents of the strong-box into a leather valise, and had carried it out with one hand with less apparent effort than most men would seem to exert if the bag were empty, although the weight had made the bottom of the valise sag out of shape.

"I'd hate to be the cop who has to tackle him," said the clerk, as he affixed the bank's seal to the empty strong-box.

The next step was to track down the taxi in which Simon Borrow had driven away, and that presented no difficulties. But before assigning a man to that job I telephoned police headquarters. They promised us "facilities" whatever those are, and my friend Casey looked in, in the course of the morning to "learn how to be a daytective" as he expressed it. He grew ribald when I showed him our condensed reports from all over the U.S.A.

"Me boy, d'ye think the State Department hasn't ten times that much dope? I could go to Washington and lay me hands on ev'ry word ye have there, only much better systematized. But suppose ye let me have a copy o' that, just for riference."

HE WAS WAITING for the copy to be typed when Brice and Allison came in, each flourishing a different news paper giving Central News accounts of Gulad's death. Allison looked heartbroken, and Brice hardly any better. Both had made their minds up that the gold plates were lost forever, and Allison was in favor of returning at once to England.

"We're discr-r-edited, disgr-r-aced, and ruined men. We found the most impor-r-tant records in the whole world, and let them be stolen from us. For pity's sake let's have the decency to retir-r-e into well-merited obleevion."

"Rot!" I answered. "We've a better chance than ever. You have the most important plate."

"Aye, ye've said the word! The key to all the others — as useless as a barren cow without the others — as useless as the lost ones are wi'out our key! Man, man; if I only knew that the thief were a scholar o' par-r-ts, I'd r-rather he'd stolen the key too than know that such invaluable witnesses o' history were rendered dumb by separ-r-ation!"

Where do ideas come from? I suppose if you could tell me that you could answer all the riddles of the universe. I was satisfied that "Simon Borrow" and Bhopal Gosh were one and the same person. And now Allison, bemoaning his disaster, provided an idea that was like a beacon on a dark night.

"We've hardly started our investigation yet," I said. "If I assure you that I've confidence in being able to recover those plates, will you stay and lend a hand?"

"Yes!" said Brice instantly. "Certainly, yes."

"Man, ye're daft!" said Allison with withering scorn. "Ye'd heap a ruinous expense on what is much too bad already! We'll gang hame to ob*lee*vion."

"I happen to be the senior member of this commission," Brice retorted quietly. "We'll stay."

Allison, yielded without another word. Brice understood him pretty thoroughly, for the two had worked together in desert places, and there is no better way to get a true line on your partner. Having made his protest as a matter of principle, Allison was only too glad to concede the point. I then propounded mine.

"The man who has taken those plates," I said, "will be as quick as anyone to recognize the value of the key to them. He has committed a murder. He'll have to stay in hiding as long as the police hue and cry lasts. He won't dare try to go aboard ship, for that's the surest way of getting caught. He's a cunning devil. The only way to catch him is to let him know that the one key-plate that completes the set and makes translation of the whole lot possible is in the United States. He'll try to get hold of it. In that way we'll get hold of him."

"Ye mean we'll use the one we have to bait a mouse-trap with?" asked Allison.

"Something like that."

"What's your plan then?" Brice demanded.

"The murder was committed, and those plates were stolen," I said, "by a man named Bhopal Gosh, a Bengali who has all along in secret been the guiding hand behind this P.O.P. He is likely to have half-a-dozen different alibis. He's a thoughtful rascal, who leaves nothing to chance but takes swift advantage of other people's carelessness. We've got to appear to be careless. We've got to parade that plate around the country in such a manner that he'll get to hear of it; and the best way we can do that, I believe, is to do it in connection with the P.O.P."

"Ye'd have a lot of black men juggling with it?" Allison demanded, shocked.

"I'd have a lot of black men discussing it," I answered. "I propose that we join the P.O.P."

"Ye mean ye'd take part in their heathenish abominations? Ye'd have us show our plate and let those black men wor-r-ship it? I'll lend idolatry no countenance on any ter-r-ms at all," snapped Allison. "The P.O.P. is a weekid schism!"

"I'll join anything, if we can get those plates back," Brice said quietly.

"Ye'll join? Then bang goes my last atom o' respect for ye!" exclaimed Allison. "Ye'll join? Oh, verra well. I recognize the adamantine nature o' y'r willfulness. I'll have to join along wi' ye, but Lord, who'd ha' thought we'd come to this!"

That being settled, I went into the next office to talk the proposal over with Strange. He already had particulars about the taxi; the driver reported having driven a "full-sized colored man," from the Cotton and Woollen National Bank as far as the Washington Square Arch, where his fare got out and mounted an uptown omnibus. That occurring to him as peculiar, he had followed the omnibus back for several blocks out of idle curiosity, and recalled its number. But that got us nowhere. A passenger with a valise can disappear from the top of an omnibus at any point he pleased along Fifth Avenue without exciting comment. Later, when I questioned the conductor he didn't as much as remember having carried him.

Chapter VIII

"He likes notes of rather large denominations."

EVENTS BEGAN TO FOLLOW now in swift succession. The first was a conference at police headquarters, by police request, in the course of which Strange and I told the whole story as far as we knew its details. The police had grilled Mrs. Aintree thoroughly, but got small change out of her. Since seeing Strange and me in the office she had executed a complete *volte face* — denied knowing much about Gulad, beyond that he returned with her party from Palestine — denied ever having seen any gold plates, although she admitted knowing that Gulad had imported "something of the sort" — had no knowledge of any one who would be likely to murder Gulad for the sake of the gold plates, but had her suspicions of a certain Mr. Brice, who Gulad had said was capable of anything and who, for all she knew, might be in New York — and was, generally speaking, indignant as well as carefully vague.

She gave the police permission to search her apartment, which they promptly did, but found nothing incriminating. The police knew nothing about Bhopal Gosh until I mentioned his name; and then knew no more of him than I did. However, within five minutes after that we had settled on a plan of action.

I went straight to Mrs. Aintree's apartment, where, in addition to one of our men in the uniform of a hall-porter, there was a pretty obvious plain-clothes policeman on duty in the vestibule. She sent out word that she was indisposed, but I answered that she could choose between interviewing me or the police, and she decided to see me alone in the room with the mirrors. She was black-angry. The creases in her forehead resembled a devil's finger-marks, and her wonderful blue eyes were alight with what I analyzed as treachery. If ever a man or woman stood ready to throw over a whole cause to save herself, that one was she — or so I read the situation.

"Have you seen the police?" I asked her.

"They have seen me. I was never more insulted in my life," she answered.

"They tell me that you deny ever having seen those gold plates," I answered.

"Can you prove that I have seen them?" she retorted. "Can you prove that they exist?"

"You're going to prove that!" I answered. "When did you last see Bhopal Gosh?"

She turned white on the instant and bit her lip.

"Who told you about Bhopal Gosh?" she answered.

"Mrs. Aintree," I said. "The police don't know — yet — that Bhopal Gosh murdered Gulad to obtain those gold plates. But I know it, and so do you. The police theory is that you were jealous of Gulad and instigated someone else to murder him. You've got one way out."

"What is it?" she demanded.

"Help bring Bhopal Gosh to book!"

She caught her breath.

"I wouldn't dare!" she answered in a hoarse voice. "I wouldn't dare!"

"You've got to dare!" I retorted. "My firm is willing to protect you. We regard you as the mere tool of Bhopal Gosh. But you've got to be frank and tell us all you know about him."

"He is the real organizer of the P.O.P.," she said, speaking almost like a woman in a dream. "He is the power behind the throne. He promised me the throne, but he was always to be the power behind it."

"I know all that," I answered, and she looked startled. There is nothing under heaven so effective as telling your informant that you know what has just been told you. They jump to the inaccurate conclusion that you knew it before they spoke.

"I d-d-daren't turn on him!" she stammered. "If he murdered Gulad, what is to stop him from murdering me?"

"I have promised you protection."

"You don't know him! He is stronger than two men, and more cunning than ten! More than cunning; he is inspired."

"By the devil?"

"Probably. To hear him talk you would believe him the greatest of philosophers. Mr. Ramsden, let that man alone! Don't drag me into this! I swear to you I had nothing whatever to do with Gulad's murder. I didn't know he had been murdered — hadn't a suspicion, until Mr. Strange telephoned this morning. This business has ruined me. I shall have to abandon my connection with the P.O.P. —"

"Why?"

"B-because of the plates," she stammered. "I am totally discredited."

"You've made arrangements to show those plates at secret meetings of the P.O.P.?"

She nodded.

"Hadn't they been shown, to anybody yet?"

"Gulad wouldn't show them. He was afraid of losing them. He was difficult to manage. He seemed to think that he was being jockeyed out of his proper place at the head of the movement. He had extraordinary fits of jealousy, and I sent for Bh—"

"Yes," I said. "Go on; you sent for Bhopal Gosh. What for?"

"I had to have advice. Bhopal Gosh was my teacher — the most resourceful man I ever knew. He came — interviewed Gulad — told me that he would manage him for me — and went away again, leaving Gulad more unmanageable than before. So I sent for another man from Boston — Pananda — a man who was my teacher formerly. But all he did was to advise me to abandon the P.O.P. I shall have to abandon it. I can't help myself."

"Pananda gave you good advice," I answered, "but you're going to undo some of the harm you've done before you just step back! You're going to help catch Bhopal Gosh!"

"I can't! I daren't!"

"Very well; come with me to police headquarters. My firm will turn its information over to the police."

"Mr. Ramsden, you don't know what you ask."

"Better than you do! I'm better able to judge the amount of harm you've done already all over the world."

"It was Bhopal Gosh, not I. Every move we made, every detail of our propaganda, has all been thought out and directed by him in advance. He had an intellect that I sometimes think is godlike, and — look at Gulad, for instance — poor Gulad, who, I suppose, refused to do his bidding! I tell you, Mr. Ramsden, that man Bhopal Gosh will get you, and get me too, if he isn't let alone! Leave him to the police! Leave me out of it!"

"You're in it already," I answered.

"Have you no pity or respect for womanhood?"

I laughed at that. I couldn't help it. Pitiable or respectable womanhood is far from the picture she presented.

"I'll protect you from Bhopal Gosh," I answered. "The point is: Will you or won't you help willingly? My time is limited."

I pulled my watch out, and I stood up. She was still hesitating.

"I must consult a lawyer."

"They'll let you see one at police headquarters. There's an officer down-stairs, who'll call a taxi if you —"

"No, no, don't do that! I'm innocent. I can prove it. Very well, Mr. Ramsden, I'll do all I can."

I sat down again and tossed my hat onto the floor.

"Have you severed your connection with the P.O.P.?" I asked.

"Not yet. There wasn't time."

"Several white members beside yourself?"

"Yes. Can't always rely on colored people to keep the real end in view. Besides, whites are quite essential when it comes to hiring halls and things like that."

"Admit three more white members."

"Who are they?"

"Brice, Allison, and myself."

"My nomination is all that would be necessary. But what is your idea?"

"Have you called off future arrangements — canceled dates for meetings — anything like that?"

"There hasn't been time. Gulad and I were scheduled to go on tour with those plates and show them in secret session to all the members everywhere."

"Don't call that off. Brice and Allison have the most important of the gold plates — the only one that wasn't stolen. You can show it and say the others are in safe-keeping. Admit some more colored members, too. I'll give you a list of their names. When are you scheduled to go on tour?"

"Wednesday of next week."

"Give me a list of the places and dates."

She took a list from her writing cabinet, and I put it in my pocket.

"I suppose your word is absolute among your followers?" I asked.

She nodded, a bit shamefacedly. It was the first sign I had seen in her of any really decent feeling.

"Contradict officially, then, any rumors about those plates

having been stolen. The story will be kept out of the newspapers if possible. If it should leak out, contradict it."

"Very well."

"And report to me instantly any effort on the part of Bhopal Gosh to get in touch with you. If he writes, don't answer him without consulting me. Will you do that?"

"Yes. But he won't try. He's far too clever."

"We'll see. Answer no questions from outsiders."

"I surely won't. I've enough trouble already."

"One more point. Until further notice, Mrs. Aintree, the power behind the throne as you have described it, of the P.O.P., will be Grim, Ramsden, and Ross! You understand me? The control has passed."

She looked daggers, but said nothing. She was not in the least convinced that she had done wrong, but regarded herself as a martyr, whose failure was due to meddlers and to circumstances over which she had no control. But she hadn't the martyr's courage, for she surrendered utterly.

I had a talk down-stairs with the man we had posted on watch, and went from there to the office on Lexington Avenue where the clerical business of the P.O.P. was done. The police had been there ahead of me, but I was permitted to make copies of the lists of foreign correspondents. There was no trace of any secret code. But there were letters that suggested a secret headquarters and an unnamed individual to whom all questions of importance, and most financial matters, were referred.

I had the lists of correspondents typed out, and mailed a copy of each to Grim and Jeremy, together with a long letter of instructions.

HAVING MAILED THOSE, the next thing was to track down as many pupils of Bhopal Gosh as possible. So I hurried back to Boston, and with some difficulty persuaded the Indian Pananda to supply me with another dozen names. The pupils whom I interviewed turned out to be in all sorts of professions. Several were extremely well-to-do. The more prosperous they were, the more highly they still seemed to think of Bhopal Gosh; a lawyer in particular was loud in his praises.

"Bhopal Gosh is a profound philosopher," he said. "He understands the law of sequence and consequence. He is a great logician. He sees behind the trivial pretenses of so-called morality, and shows those whom he teaches how to avail themselves of universal laws, in business and in other ways."

"He has made money for you?" I suggested.

"My prosperity is due to his teaching."

"Have you made any money for him?"

The lawyer hesitated. "I may say I've had several dealings with him — eminently satisfactory, all above board and, from a financial standpoint, amazing."

"Do you know his present whereabouts?"

"No. He has discontinued teaching. Things he taught went to the heads of immature individuals, some of whom got into serious trouble; but that was not his fault. I haven't heard from him for weeks."

I found three of the ex-pupils in the penitentiary.

"I'm a crook," said one of them. "I pleaded guilty. But I wouldn't have been a crook except for that man. I paid him two hundred and fifty dollars for a course of lessons in how to be dishonest without being found out. That's all it amounted to. I was found out. I'm glad I was caught before it got worse."

The other two were even more indignant. One of them stated his intention of "laying for" Bhopal Gosh as soon as he was free again.

"The man taught what isn't so. He had two hundred and fifty dollars of my money, and I got five years. He's going to get eternity when I get out of this — you watch!"

The prosperous pupils were all full of his praises. The disappointed ones — and there were several — all swore he was an arch-impostor who taught dishonesty as other men teach chemistry or mathematics.

"And it's the hardest thing in the world to forget his teachings," one of them asserted. She was, a woman, by the way.

"He makes you believe that black is white by calling it gray and then leading you on by one step at a time. You catch yourself forever afterwards hesitating between right and wrong, wondering whether wrong really is as bad as it's painted."

None of them knew Bhopal Gosh's present whereabouts, not even the prosperous ones, all of whom admitted having let their teacher "stand in" with them from time to time in some successful deal or other.

"Why not?" was their invariable comment.

Bhopal Gosh had run no risks. He had taught a sort of hairline course of crookedness, and left his pupils free to follow it. When they succeeded he fattened on their sense of gratitude. When they failed he let them go to jail. Until he murdered Gulad apparently he had let others take the whole responsibility while he shared profits only. From that time on the chase began to assume a new phase. Hitherto it had been a sort of intellectual problem, but now all my old hunter's instincts came to the surface, and I set out to finish Bhopal Gosh as personally keen on the job as if he had been a man-eating tiger. I made no bones about it. Didn't deceive myself. Gold plates or no gold plates, I was out to get my man.

THAT HE WASN'T GOING to be easy to get became more and more evident as I looked over the latest reports of the case in the New York office. Inquiries had revealed the fact, for instance, that he had no passport in the name of Bhopal Gosh, but that for more than three years a Bengali named Lajpat Shuddi had constantly renewed one, and the photograph attached to Lajpat Shuddi's application blank bore a striking resemblance to that of the alleged negro Simon Borrow. Ergo, Lajpat Shuddi, Simon Borrow, and Bhopal Gosh were one and the same individual, and likely to prove an uncommonly elusive trinity.

That he was at large and in full possession of self-confidence was made clear while I was reading that dossier. The man I had left on duty phoned in to say that Mrs. Aintree had just had a long-distance call from Chicago. He had been interfered with while trying to listen in; some of her "meek ones" had come down-stairs and practically driven him away from the switchboard. However, he had found out that the call came from a public pay-station somewhere within the Loop.

I hurried around. Mrs. Aintree lied sturdily at first — said the call was from a friend in Springfield, Massachusetts, who was sick and wanted to borrow money. But she wilted when I threatened her with the police again.

"I'm not guessing," I assured her. "I know you had a call from Chicago. Was it Bhopal Gosh?"

She nodded.

"What did he say?"

"Mr. Ramsden, I won't — I daren't repeat it."

"Why not?"

"He forbade me!"

"Very well. You're helping him to escape the clutches of the law. I'll call in the police."

"Mr. Ramsden, I am not helping him! He is not guilty! He called up to tell me about the murder. He said it was unfortunate that the plates had been stolen, and that the murderer was probably too smart for the police. However, he said he is confident of finding the man, and meanwhile he himself feels that it will be wisest to lie low, both because suspicion may rest on him mistakenly at present, and also because he will stand a better chance in that way of catching the real culprit."

"Did you tell him there's a warrant out against him?"

"Yes."

"You promised me you wouldn't answer any communication from him without consulting me first!"

"I couldn't help it," she answered with rising anger. "You don't know that man! I do know him! I have a perfect right to tell him there is a warrant out for his arrest. Perhaps he will surrender to the police. Who knows!"

"My ye-e-es! Who knows! Did you tell him anything about the other gold plate?"

"No. He asked whether the P.O.P. members knew that the plates had been stolen, and I told him 'no.' Then he said a little ingenuity would show me some way out of the predicament of having no plates to show to the members, and that he might send me a suggestion before long."

"What else?"

"No more. He rang off then."

"Has he ever sent you any money?" I demanded.

"Once. A sum to cover expenses."

"How did he send it? Check — draft — money-order — letter of credit?"

"In hundred-dollar bills by registered mail."

"From what postoffice?"

"I don't know. I threw the envelope away."

"When was it that he sent you money?"

"About three weeks ago."

"Have you ever seen his check?"

"Never. All the payments I have ever seen him make were in bills."

"Have you ever paid money to him?"

"Often. I have turned over contributions to him."

"Cash or check?"

"Cash, always. He likes notes of rather large denominations."

"Are those transactions shown on any book?"

"I don't know. I suppose so. He keeps the secret books himself."

"Don't you know where he banks the money?"

"No."

That closed another avenue of search effectually. The banks are thoroughly organized among themselves for mutual protection, and more crooks are caught with their aid than in any other way, but it was safe to say that we would have to run down Bhopal Gosh without the banks' assistance.

CHAPTER IX

"And if they all offers me a li'l sweet'nin', Cap'n?"

DOWN ON THE southern deserts of this country there is a reptile they call the Sidewinder. He's a rattlesnake by habit, history, and profession, and seems to like it, not having changed his habits since the first Conquistadores came. His chief characteristic is that he invariably heads south when traveling west. Besides, he carries a rattle on his tail, packs a murderous disposition and has all the other rattlesnake peculiarities.

We became Sidewinders. We had Mrs. Aintree, basking hardly in the sun but in the limelight of importance. She would have been happy on the gallows if only a fair-sized crowd were there to stare at her. We carried that gold plate along, with the idea of rattling it until every darky and most of the white folks in the towns we visited should be aware of it, and us. Our party pretty nearly filled a Pullman car, which made a fine long snake of us, of assorted colors. And we headed south while traveling west. The murderous disposition was a poor thing, but mine own; and by way of fangs we had some Smith & Wessons straight from the factory in Springfield.

The car that we engaged, and that Meldrum Strange paid for, was one of those steel composite affairs with sets of drawing-rooms at either end and regulation Pullman berths in the middle. So there was plenty of accommodation for Mrs. Aintree and her party at one end, Brice, Allison, myself and three other white men at the other, and our dusky confraternity amidships, so to speak.

They were about as fine a collection of U.S. darkies as you could assemble anywhere. Some had been to college; some had worked for banks and suchlike institutions; some had been the rounds of vaudeville, and half a dozen of them had rustled soft coal in the bowels of foreign-going ships. We knew all about every one of them from the day he was born; more than they thought we knew in certain instances — for example, that our middle-weight prize-fighter and cleverest corner-man had served a term in jail — and we had every one deeded up as a full-fledged member of the P.O.P. They ranked as "aspirants," in good standing, subscription paid, and knew the secret ritual by heart; in fact they invented quite a lot of new stuff on the train, for the benefit of small-town hicks who hadn't yet received the latest light.

Brice turned out to be a splendid traveling companion, and Allison a tolerable one, although Allison could see no humor in the business, and was much more exercised over the expense than Meldrum Strange, who had to stay in New York but was paying for it all.

"Man, the ineequity upsets ma' mind. It's a blasphemous and beastly or-r-ganization run by the very hoore o' Babylon hersel'. That's bad enough. But we add the offense o' squanderin' dollars as if money weren't the verra blood that should be cir-r-culating in the veins o' 'ceevilization!"

He regarded every man with us as a religious renegade, and himself as the worst of all.

"Brice is a pagan — I've long had ma doots o' Brice — a good, brave little body but a her-r-etic in matters o' rel*ee*gion. I rue the day I said I'd go with ye on this exped*ee*tion, but a man's wor-r-d is his wor-r-d, and there's no takin' it back. But Lord forgie us!"

He was the sort of man who would have endured the rack a couple of centuries ago rather than yield on the interpretation of some obscure Greek particle in one of Paul's Epistles — the kind of man who came over to this continent and founded a new nation out of guts, resource, and pure pig-headedness. He went in fear of Hell that whole long journey, solely from a sense of duty and determination not to be outdone by Brice. He reminded us of our sins a little too frequently, but he kept us awake by preaching when we should have been asleep, and that, as it happened, provided us with the clue that solved the problem in the end.

ONE OF THE MEMBERS of Mrs. Aintree's party — the meekest of them all and the most obsequious in looking after her — was a man named Carter. According to Brice he was the individual who had told Grim too much in Jerusalem and so had started our investigation rolling. He had made up for it since by the most painstaking discretion; in fact, he. seemed afraid to comment on the weather without getting Mrs. Aintree's permission first. He was a silver-haired man, somewhere between fifty and sixty, who always wore a black morning coat and carefully creased trousers, but economized on pocket-handkerchiefs.

He had a way of walking about the car, treading cat-wise, making no noise, and if ever we left the door of our drawing-room open he would trip past two or three times, glancing in, smiling and saying something pleasant if we noticed him, but, if we didn't notice him, only too glad to get by without saying anything at all. I won't say he aroused our suspicions, because after the event you always think you were suspicious from the first; that's human nature. We told one another we had suspected him, but I'm inclined to believe that we fooled ourselves on that score.

Allison refused to sleep in a compartment by himself because he had the gold plate in his satchel, and Brice, being rather tired of him in some ways, begged me to take turns sharing the responsibility. So the first night out Allison and I slept together, and Brice alone; but there was a door between the two compartments that we left unlocked. Brice, having nothing to worry about, and not being a nervous sort of man, forgot to lock the other door of his compartment leading into the corridor. Brice was in compartment A, in which the three of us had sat talking all the afternoon. I had the upper berth in compartment B, and Allison the lower, with the satchel under his pillow; and for a long time after we put the lights out Allison lay underneath, me, quoting pessimistic verses from the Book of the Lamentations of Jeremiah.

Now I'm not a miserable-minded man.

It gets my goat to have to listen too long to a sermon on original sin. I believe in original decency — monkeys are perhaps descended from man, for instance, certainly not man from monkeys — just as I believe in original gold in the everlasting hills. The only thing I ever knew, except toothache, that could make me sleepless is just such a sermon on the baseness of the human race as Allison got off his chest that night.

So I lay awake, listening to Brice's snoring and wishing that Allison hadn't set his suit-case so as to keep the door from closing by about an inch. But I was too lazy to get down and move the thing.

It was about midnight when I heard the door of Brice's compartment open softly. For a moment I thought it was Brice on the prowl. But he snored on, and I heard the door click shut again, as if some pussy-foot had sneaked in. Then Allison, fast asleep, started pitching about as if undergoing in imagination all the torments foretold by Jeremiah. I took advantage of that disturbance to get down from the upper berth without making much noise, and instead of opening the door between the two compartments, which would only have scared the intruder into flight, I slipped out into the corridor through the door of compartment B, closed it behind me, and walked forward to the door of compartment A.

I moved the latch, and let the door swing open as if the intruder hadn't fastened it behind him and the motion of the train had done the rest — then stood back in the dimly lighted corridor and looked in.

It was our white-haired acquaintance Carter, black morning coat and all. He heard the door swing open, but I was in time to see him withdraw his hand from under Brice's pillow. He started to close the door again, and actually had his hand on it when he caught sight of me.

Now I've met with gall from Maine to Shanghai, all the way around the earth and back again — all sorts, all grades, and all degrees; but nothing to equal his. I guess you've got to be meek before you can think of such a thesis as he propounded.

"I came to stop Mr. Brice from snoring," he said. "He's annoying Mrs. Aintree."

Mrs. Aintree's compartment was at the front end of the car, at least fifty feet away, and between ours and hers were thirty colored men, putting up among them such a saw-mill chorus as you'd never hear anywhere outside of a lumber camp or a *kraal* in Africa. I pushed him back into Brice's compartment and turned the light on, locking the door behind me.

"Well, really!" he exclaimed; and Brice woke up with a start.

THE NEXT THING, ALLISON came stalking through the communicating door with an old-fashioned dueling-pistol cocked in front of him. In his pajamas, with that pained, intense expression on his face and his long nose following the pistol's aim, he looked like one of those cartoons of a Frenchman hunting sparrows that they used to print in England when Fashoda was the main topic of discussion. I asked him to put the pistol away, for I've seen accidents happen with those things; but he wouldn't listen to me.

"Well, really!" remarked the silver-haired intruder for the second time.

"Ye'll know it's real when ye've a bullet in ye!" answered Allison. "Disar-r-m the man, one of ye!"

You might as well have talked about disarming an old woman. If he had had a weapon — and he had none — it would have been perfectly safe to leave him in possession of it. He wasn't exactly frightened, he was more like Daniel in the lion's den, obedient to what he considered first principles and confident that some way of escape would open out — a much more difficult kind of man to deal with than the blustering sort, who always throw their hands up when weapons fail.

"Sit down in that corner," I said, "and tell us what you were looking for under Brice's pillow. I saw your hand under it."

"The chiel was sear-r-ching for the gold plate!" put in Allison contemptuously. "That answer's too obvious to need confir-r-mation."

"Let me go, please," said our unwilling guest. "I am a member of this party with a perfectly legal right to come and go in the car as I please. I came in here to stop this gentleman from snoring. Let me go, please."

Allison swore under his breath. Brice looked at me whimsically.

"Did Mrs. Aintree send you on this errand?" I demanded.

"She couldn't sleep. She asked me to do what I could about it."

An idea occurred to me that instant. If you call it intuition, that doesn't explain what intuition is, any more than calling the differential calculus a method of fluxions brings you closer to an understanding of it.

"You'd better get out of here," I said. "Knock next time you've any message to deliver!"

He walked out without comment, and I slammed the door behind him, opening it again instantly and stepping out into the corridor to watch. He never once looked back. The impression I got was that he was hurrying to reach his own end of the car before he should be seen by someone else. If that was so he didn't make it.

As he passed midway down the car the curtain of a lower berth drew back, and a kinky, dusky head appeared. It wasn't curiosity that drew that head out, but conspiracy. The difference in expression of those two emotions is far too wide to permit of a mistake. Carter appeared disconcerted — really disconcerted for the first time — whispered something hurriedly, and passed on. The kinky head grinned and retired inside the curtains, but only for a minute, for as soon as Carter had regained his own compartment I went and pulled those curtains aside again.

"Sam!"

"Thah?"

He had two false front teeth, which he removed at night, and couldn't speak at that hour without lisping.

"Follow me down to compartment A."

He struggled into his overcoat, looking more like a chimpanzee than a human, although owning a good-natured grin that offset certain other peculiarities. His pug nose resembled a dark piece of india-rubber and looked as if you could punch it steadily for an hour or two without causing its owner much inconvenience. He had a retreating jaw that must have been hard to hit in the prize-ring, and one cauliflower ear. Nevertheless, his bright little eyes gleamed with unusual intelligence, as I backed him up against the door of our compartment.

"D'you want to get back into the Federal prison, Sam?"

"Don't know nothin' about no Federal prithon, thah."

"Well, I do know. Your term was reduced to two years and eight months for good behavior. You came out exactly a year and eleven months ago. The point is, d'you want to get in again?"

"Cap'n, how come you athk me that? Good conduc's ma middle name. Ah signed on thith heah outfit jes' cause you-all said as you wanted a good conduc' fightin' man. Ah's good conduc', an' —"

"Certainly. You were living straight, so we decided to give you a chance."

"That wath thertainly good of you-all, Cap'n."

"Well then, why don't you reciprocate?"

"Rethiprocate, thah? Ah don't 'zac'ly get youah meanin'?"

"Does Mr. Carter, or does Mrs. Aintree know that you've been in jail?"

"Mithith Aintree, she knowth it, thah."

"How did she find it out?"

"Cap'n, thay, it wath she what put me in! It was she what had me 'rested in the futht inthtanth."

"I see. So she came to you now with a proposal?"

"If you all want to call what she thaid a propothal, thath mebbe youah senthe o' humor, Cap'n. Ah'd call it a threat, Ah would, jes' like that."

"Out with it! What did she say?"

"Thaid Ah might do her a thmall favor, an' 'lowed she'd do me a big 'un."

"Wouldn't let on about having been in jail, I suppose?"

"That it, thah, Cap'n, 'zac'ly. 'F Ah'd send her li'l telegram by-um-by, thoon as she gives the word to let 'er go, she'll say nothin' 'bout my unfortunate ekthperienthe."

"Telegram to whom?"

"Dunno, Cap'n, thah. Not seen it yet."

"Where were you to send it from?"

"Thome thathion along the line, Cap'n."

"Cautioned you to say nothing about it?"

"Shoah did."

"Why didn't you come and tell me?"

"Cap'n, thah, you-all nevah said no word to me 'bout not thendin' no telegrams."

"That's true. That clears you."

"Goo'night, Cap'n!"

"Wait a minute! Did Mr. Carter have anything to say about that telegram?"

"No, thah."

"Then what were you expecting from him when he returned along the car just now?"

"Ah don't 'xac'ly know, Cap'n. Mithter Carter, he thaid, Mithith Aintree'th order, an' he'd go t'your compartment 'long about thith time an' get a li'l package f'r me to keep, an' along come mo'ning he'd tell me what to do with it. Mebbe ordahs 'ud be for me to take it off'n train an' go thomewheres, but he'd let me know 'bout that. Then he come 'long an' ain't got no parthel, an' he look tho dithappointed I come mighty near laffin' in his face."

IT SOUNDED TRUE. Sam Carson had fallen foul of the Mann Act, which like many other laws unavoidably lends itself to blackmail and occasional injustice.

When Strange investigated Sam's references and discovered that he had been in jail, even the deputy prosecuting attorney who had secured Sam's conviction admitted that there might have been a miscarriage of justice. He had eloped into another state with Mrs. Aintree's colored maid at a time when he had a fairly large cash forfeit posted for a match against one of the most notorious ring-sharpers in the game, and the combination of circumstances had been too strong for him.

The woman was persuaded to accuse him, partly by Mrs.

Aintree, who resented the inconvenience of losing her personal maid, and partly by the men who stood to keep Sam's forfeit money if he should fail to appear at the ring-side.

Sam may have told the truth when he pleaded not guilty at his trial, and I was pretty nearly certain that he was telling the exact truth to me that night.

"All right, Sam," I said. "Take anything they give you. If they give you a telegram, get off the train and send it."

" 'F you thay tho, Cap'n."

"D'you think you could make a copy of it first?"

"Ah ain't no writin' expert, Cap'n. Fightin's ma peculiarity," he answered with a grin.

"Can you read?"

"Yeth thah, Ah can read good."

"Have you a good memory?"

"Ah can 'member mos' ev'rythin' ever happened."

"If they were to give you a telegram, and you were to read it over twenty or thirty times, d'you think you could memorize the whole of it?"

"Ah's a fus'-class memorizer. Ah 'members the 'zac' wo'din' o' the telegram 'at Jack Johnson send to his ole mother, time he knock the stuffin' out o' Misto' Jeff at Reno. Ah 'members —"

"That'll do. The most interesting part of their telegram will be the name and address of the party it's sent to. Get that into your head so you'll remember it a thousand years, if you live that long. Then remember as much of the rest as possible. D'you get me?"

"Ah'll do ma bes', Cap'n. Anything to 'blige."

"That's all, except hold your tongue. Don't say a word to a soul about your talk in here with me tonight."

"An' if they all offers me a li'l sweetnin', Cap'n?"

"Take it. But no blackmail, mind! You're not to ask them for a cent. If they give you nothing, go ahead and send the telegram just the same. There are no side-pickings on this trip, unless you get hurt in a scrap later on, and in that case we'll take care of you. Are you all clear on that?"

"All cleah, Cap'n. Goo'night, thah. Goo'night, gents."

He went off looking like a scarecrow in an overcoat with sleeves much too short for his long arms. Delight in being on the inside of conspiracy made him do a sort of double-shuffle down between the berths, and huge hands' flapping at the ends of loose arms heightened the illusion. But he made good on the memory test.

They left us on a side-track at a wayside junction in Virginia in the early morning, and we had to stay there until nearly noon before a local "mixed" rolled in and they hitched us to its rear end en route for Appleton. Our gang piled out to invade the short-order places that stood three in a row within fifty yards of the depot, and that gave Mrs. Aintree the perfect opportunity. None of her party left the car, but Brice, Allison, and I watched Sam go lolloping off toward the Western Union office, and presently he came back toward us muttering to himself.

We let him keep on muttering. It wasn't in the game to let the Aintree party know that we suspected them of using Sam to upset our calculations. He looked well-paid and satisfied, and sat in the car with his feet on the seat in front of him, moving his lips like a monk at prayer, until a crap game started at the Aintree end, and what with one disturbance and another it looked safe enough to send for him to our compartment.

He stood with his back to the door, his enormous feet together, and his hands behind his back, displaying two removable gold teeth in a grin like a souvenir of Halloween, and rattled off his piece as though he went by clockwork and had been over-wound or something.

"MistoAntonioVittoriRDThreeLakelockCalDon'tPhoneS endByMessengerMessagePrepaidCostOfMessengerCollectD ayLetter. XpectUsMiddleNextWeekSparksOrLittleLa terWillTryWireYouXacDateArrivalButAllCorrespondence DangerousAt PresentStopMissingThirtySecondPlateAccom paniedInChargeRamsdenBriceAllisonAllWhiteAlertSus piciousAdviseUtmostCautionStopThis InformationSent YouConditionalYourReciprocityStopWill RenderAllPos sibleAssistanceDespiteGraveRiskButExpectYouIncludeMeI nAnyFuturePlanOfCampaignAndConsiderYou Hardly InPositionToRefuseStopConsiderPOPNowWorthless Per sonSuperintendingThisTripEvidentlyHasPlanToUpsetAll HasMillionaireBackingAndWillDoJobThoroughlyStopBeSu re GetInTouchSparksTakingAllConceivablePrecaution SignedYourPupil."

"What name and address were on the bottom of the telegram?" I asked him.

"CarolineWattsNineWestTwentyThirdStreetNewYork City, thah."

Well, with the aid of a pencil and paper, and by dint of making

Sam repeat the message over and over, it took about twenty minutes to make sense of it all. He couldn't remember it unless he said it quickly, and when he said it quickly it was totally impossible to understand him. To him it seemed to have no meaning anyhow, except that he had been told to keep the change out of a twenty-dollar bill. However, we got the hang of it finally, and let him go forward, well-pleased with himself.

Nor was Sam the only person who was pleased. If the telegram meant anything at all, it was that Bhopal Gosh's alibi and present address were now in my possession. I had never heard of Lakelock, but knew that Sparks is in Nevada, so it was fair to presume that Lakelock was somewhere near.

Caroline Watts was clearly the *nom de plume* of Mrs. Aintree. Antonio Vittori was equally certainly Bhopal Gosh. If I could once catch sight of the brute I didn't doubt I could corner him, so I decided to make Appleton, and after that to cancel all the rest of the schedule and head straight for Sparks, Nevada.

CHAPTER X

"Res egaliter omnibus!"

IT WAS NEARLY DARK when we arrived at Appleton, among bleak hills that had been stripped of trees. There were a few truck gardens, the inevitable roped cows, unthrifty-looking goats by the dozen, and of course pigs, but nothing that resembled farming. It looked like one of those places that import everything in tin cans, milk included, and the empty cans made up most of the scenery.

Yet it wasn't such a small place. It had evidently spread during the war, and had begun to dwindle subsequently. All the straggling, outlying parts of the town consisted of mere shacks, no longer painted, and inhabited exclusively by colored folk, who had come there for wartime wages and remained because it was the easiest thing to do. There were rows and rows of empty cottages, and the white folks' houses, on a hill at one end of the town, wore a deserted look, as did most of the mines, although the pit-head gear in places appeared to be in working order.

Take it on the whole, Appleton was as perfect a place as you could find for brewing discontent. You could hardly be happy there if you tried, what with falling wages, falling population, falling houses, trade, ambition, everything. Mrs. Aintree pointed out her home — a large frame house on a hill-top, standing in considerable grounds, but empty, and I didn't wonder that she lacked desire to live in it. She said that her late husband had controlled half the mines in the place, but the coal was low-grade stuff and hardly paid for mining any longer.

Mrs. Aintree had engaged the town hall ten days in advance, and the place was placarded with notices of a P.O.P. revival meeting that evening "for members and their friends;" but I turned our gang loose through the town to do a little word-of-mouth advertisement, and, having sat idle in the train so long, they were eating their heads off for mischief. The advance announcements of Noah's Flood probably sounded something like the news they spread through Appleton.

Mrs. Aintree seized opportunity to mail a letter. She said it was to her friend in Springfield, but she wore her dark look as she spoke, and I knew she was lying. The postmistress wouldn't give me any information, so I wrote a short letter myself to Meldrum Strange and registered it. While the postmistress copied the address into her book I got a look at the previous entry, and — as I expected — it bore the name of Antonio Vittori, Lakelock, California.

That was perfectly satisfactory. However quickly we might get away from Appleton, it was a certainty that mail would reach the border of California ahead of us, for our car would be hitched on to local trains and dandled to a dead march across the continent. The more time Antonio Vittori Bhopal Gosh should have to mature his plans, the more likely he would be to fall into our trap. Mrs. Aintree had served the purpose so far perfectly. It would be time for her to send another telegram a day or so before our premature arrival on the scene. So I didn't tell her anything about our change of schedule until after we left Appleton next morning, and Sam received private instructions in the meantime. When she did give him a telegram he kept it in his pocket until I gave the word to send it off.

The P.O.P. was a platform for her self-esteem and no more. She cared nothing for the disappointment of her dupes. Only her own predicament disturbed her seriously, and she believed that her only port in the storm was partnership with Bhopal Gosh, the man who had supplied the brains from the beginning. She realized as well as I did that the one gold plate we had with us would be an irresistible temptation to the man who had the other thirty-one.

Bhopal Gosh probably knew Sanskrit. If so, he could appreciate and probably had told her that the stolen thirty-one plates were unintelligible without the thirty-second, the key plate. He probably told her in imaginative oriental phrases how stupendously important the complete set would be; and as a matter of plain fact he could hardly have exaggerated. The original law of Moses, engraved on gold, could be used to produce a more effective world upheaval than any scrap of paper signed at

Versailles. Consider what the Mormons did, and are doing. What Mohammed did. And there are others.

Mrs. Aintree had faith in Bhopal Gosh and his adroit intellect. She trusted him to contrive some means of stealing it. Her one remaining chance of wielding the world-wide influence she craved was to help Bhopal Gosh and then, if necessary, blackmail him. Otherwise her folly in consenting to make the journey with us in that car would be inexplicable.

Money did not appeal to her much except as a means to a definite end. The end that she never lost sight of, was self-importance. She yearned to be looked up to — admired — reverenced. She was willing to go through anything, to compromise to any extent, to condone any wickedness with specious argument, provided only that her own sense of importance should be bolstered in the end. And Bhopal Gosh, who knew that side of human nature, being built of just such stuff himself, understood, and laughed at her, as the sequel proved.

Of course, this is *ex-post-facto* analysis. It is extremely easy to deceive yourself when looking backward and imagine you were wise about it all from the beginning. The truth is that I had some uncommonly discouraged moments and, for instance, while we were waiting for our evening entertainment I went and interviewed the chief of the Appleton police. I took him quite a long way into confidence.

IT WAS A HECTIC EVENING from the start, for Darktown turned out and filled the hall long before we got there. According to the chief of police there had been nearly a score of free-lance agitators in the town during the past few weeks, every one of whom had left a standing grouch behind him.

So they were ready to be preached to. They wanted to be told that heaven lay just beyond the hill and could be reached by revolution. We had our own men scattered about the hall before it filled, and one or two of them made alleged impromptu speeches before the opening ceremony, with the idea of keeping good humor as near the surface as possible; for it was a risky game we were going to play — the sort of game that follows better on a joke or two than on solemnity.

Our fellows had the ritual down fine, and had even improved on it. It had mostly been designed by Mrs. Aintree with a view to the superstitious appeal, and in order to lend solemnity to her ridiculous pretensions. For instance, after a dreamy hymn, there was a solemn parade around the hall in Indian file, each man doing the lock-step with his hands on the shoulders of him in front; that was supposed to represent the wanderings of Israelites in the wilderness for forty years, and it might have gone right well on this occasion if our men hadn't interjected *sotto voce* jokes reminiscent of the A.E.F. One laugh led to another, and they drowned out the piano finally by singing the old songs that some of them had howled in France.

So by the time Mrs. Aintree entered, pompous as a peacock with her staff around her, they were ready for pretty nearly anything except serious business. We had ten trumpeters, who represented the Israelitish heralds sounding the blast that blew down the walls of Jericho. Five trumpeters stood on each side of the door, as she entered surrounded by meek white minions and followed at a decent distance by Brice and Allison carrying the gold plate framed upright on a tea-tray. I came last and received an ovation, although I did not know why until Sam informed me afterwards that he had advertised me as the "champeen heavy-weight long-distance African golfer of the whole wide world."

At the sound of the first blast they all got to their feet. There were five more blasts while Mrs. Aintree strode up the aisle magnificently, at each of which they were supposed to shout: "Glory Hallelujah! The kingdom is at hand!" By the seventh blast Mrs. Aintree had reached the platform and they all sat down, throwing one leg over the other to signify that the walls had fallen and that all they had to do now was to enjoy the feasting and the loot.

There was quite an obvious difference between members and their friends. Members knew which leg to throw over which, for instance — a very important point. They also knew the responses, and were all the more readily tickled into ribald laughter by the new ones interjected by our men.

Mrs. Aintree came to the front of the platform, and stood there holding up a hand for silence. But silence was a long time coming. Circumstances were against her. The tattered old crimson canvas drop-curtain had not been raised to the full distance, and she stood exactly underneath the daubed, recumbent undraped figure of a fat and silly-looking Bacchus, engaged in pouring a stream of yellow wine out of a blue cornucopia. He was leering down at her. It was only a matter of seconds, apparently, before the stream of wine would splash on her head. The audience refused to stop laughing until somebody went behind and raised the curtain to its full height. Then —

"What is the sacred number?" she demanded in ringing tones.

"Seven!" they answered.

"Come eleven!" shouted one of our men, and a roar of laughter greeted that, which she did her best to ignore.

"Oh you little lucky, lovely, rollin' bones!" said someone with a bass voice like a bull's, and that pretty nearly brought the house down. However, she continued —

"How many are the tenets of the P.O.P.?"

"Seven!" they answered.

"What are they?" she went on instantly, giving nobody a chance to interpose a joke.

The reply sounded like a Sunday-school class reciting the catechism in quick time:

> *"Brotherly love for all black races,*
> *Brotherly blacks in 'portant places,*
> *Wilderness once crossed is over,*
> *Tired ones have a right to clover,*
> *Handsome is as handsome does,*
> *Whatever is good is good for us,*
> ***Res egaliter omnibus!"***

(Even dog-Latin, you see, to give it a properly scholarly flavor.)

"Ah's agwine ride in dat omnibus!" some one shouted from the rear of the hall. "No moah flat-footin' them ole deserts! Ah's hit them ties too off en! Hee-hee! Ah's agwine ride!"

"Getup!" yelled someone else.

"No, chillun, this heah's a motor-bus. Ain't agwine be no mewls this trip!"

"Honk-honk! Ting-a-ling! Pah-pah! Who ain't paid his fare?"

Mrs. Aintree tried to laugh it off good-naturedly, but her anger was rising. Her frown betrayed her, and the audience realized that perfectly. They set themselves deliberately to annoy her, and succeeded beyond their wildest expectations.

She tried to make a speech, but they interrupted with corner-man remarks. The more she tried to browbeat them with eloquence, the worse they got out of hand, egged on by our conspirators strategically posted to produce the most effect.

"My friends!" she began. "I have brought you a surprise from

New York — or rather from beneath the sands of ancient Egypt."

"Ah trembles wid antiquity! Oh, hold ma hand!"

"You were promised the privilege of feasting your eyes on the thirty-one plates —"

"Wi' turkey on um, an' sweets, an' gra-avy — Oh you Tha-a-nksgivin'! Show me them eats!"

"— but we have a greater privilege in store for you tonight. Instead of bringing the thirty-one plates that were promised, and which would have been a cumbersome and difficult thing to do —"

"Not 'nuff room in dat ole omnibus! Plates no use anyhaow widout knives an' forks! Yah-hah! Mebbe 'Gyptians didn't use no knives an' forks. Fingers plenty good 'nough for them 'Gyptians!"

"— we have brought you the most wonderful thing in the world — the veritable key plate — drafted by the hand of Moses himself — the original Moses — think of it! — and bearing a portrait of Moses done by an artist of his day, engraved on the original solid gold plate on which, in Sanskrit, an ancient tongue, are inscribed the key words by which, with proper understanding, the secret, mystic, marvelous writings on the other thirty-one may be interpreted!"

She paused for breath, and they were really silent for the first time. That was quite a bomb to spring on any audience, and there was quite a number of them in the hall who had been sufficiently filled beforehand with a sense of the seriousness of what they called their Pisgah Vision to have won the rest over, had she known enough to keep their attention fixed on the treasure, instead of redirecting it toward herself. But she was so constituted that she couldn't help herself, being quite capable of being jealous of an inanimate object if that should detract for half-a-minute from her own importance.

"Since I ceased to live among you," she resumed, "being called elsewhere to higher duties —"

"Leaky ole roof needs mendin' — wouldn't spen' 'nuff dollars on de ole roof, that's what!"

"Tenant, he's gone too! He said, '— ole house not fit for man to live in!' He va-a-moose an' pay no rent!"

"Some's been dug all the taters out o' tater patch. Yeah! No more taters!"

"Win'ows all bus' in! House begins look like he's ha'nted!"

"Rats in dat ole house bigger'n possums! O-o-oh!"

"— I have always had a kindly feeling — more, a passion in my heart for Appleton —"

"Doggone ole slag-heap ain't got no passion lef'. Kiss muh, honey Appleton, an' say goo'bye! Ah's gwine follow whar Lady Luck done up an' went — she's mah beau!"

"— and therefore it is you, from out of all the hosts of lodges of the P.O.P., who are the first to set your eyes on this priceless heirloom of the centuries!"

"Oooh! Our eyes ache lookin' at yuh, honey boy! Moses, yo' sho' resembles Lady Luck's gen'lem'n frien'! Ooey! You is good to see!"

"Dawgonnit! Dat stuff's yaller go-o-old! You-all done hear dat, niggahs?"

I patted my hip-pocket, which was bulging rather ostentatiously as I stood at the end of the line next to Brice and Allison, who were holding the tray between them. Allison nudged me and moved his lips as if I were responsible for the safety of his only child, and for a moment I feared he intended to snatch up the plate and decamp with it, which would have started a riot almost certainly. But in the pause that followed the last negro's remark, Mrs. Aintree swept into her stride once more. She was full of courage of a kind, that woman, and not minded to be laughed out of countenance.

"But you seem to be in an impudent mood tonight," she went on. "Some spirit of unrest has made you forget your manners. You seem inclined to overlook the fact that I have come all the way from New York at tremendous cost and inconvenience to show you what many other men — and white folks too! — would almost give their eyes to see! I find you in no mood of reverence. The years I spent among you, teaching, must have had effect, but tonight you forget yourselves! I bear no malice; but I see no humor in your stupid jests, and you certainly can't expect me to stand here and talk to you unless my words fall on properly attentive ears."

"We's lis'nin', honey! We's de lis'nin'est folks what is!"

"Yah-hoo! Mah haid's stuff' up wiv lis'nin', an' I ain't heard nuffin' yet!"

"Silence! Order! Niggah, shut yo' mouf!"

"And so I think it better for tonight that one of your own people should address you. Perhaps you'll give him a more attentive hearing. Perhaps when you realize how deeply one of your own people is impressed by the sacredness and vast importance of this relic that you are being privileged to see — perhaps then you will listen to him more respectfully and try to show your appreciation of the unheard-of good fortune that is yours tonight."

She stepped back a pace or two, and one of my men at the back of the stage produced a chair for her. Allison and Brice took chairs as well, but I didn't care to sit down, for I knew what was coming, more or less, and the others didn't — least of all Mrs. Aintree, who supposed I had provided a speaker capable of undoing the P.O.P. with faint praise. But my man stepped forward from the rear with a grin on his face that might have disillusioned her if she hadn't been paying so much attention to the set of her skirts. He was a big, stout darky — a college graduate — who had spent most of his time trying to force his way on to the legitimate stage, earning his living meanwhile in small-town vaudeville, with occasional side-excursions as a member of a quartette and, now and then when times were bad, a spell of ballyhooing for a one-ring circus. He had a magnificent baritone voice, and was not only dressed in evening clothes, which suited his ambition finely, but was drawing the best pay he had ever come in contact with outside dreamland — Tom Tulliver by name, as decent and as clean-living a colored man as I want to have any dealings with, and an expert in the psychology of his own race, as well as a born actor.

"FOLKS!" HE BEGAN, and if he had been a white man with burned cork on he could have held any audience after that first word. "I wuz agwine to call you jokes, but you-all ain't funny enough for that. You ain't got 'nuff 'nthusiasm to crank a car with. You ain't aware o' all your opportunities, what stands heah starin' yo' in the face, an' you all gapin' back at 'em wiv eyes as bright an' lively as fried aigs stuck on yo' faces!

"This heah's an epoch, that's what this is — an epoch up an' beck'nin' yo'. And an epoch is as diff'runt from a shepoch as di'monds is from the loser's end of a game o' crap. You've all met up wiv shepochs; there ain't no use o' my standin' heah tellin' you 'at shepochs ain't no good. Ah'd be a-wastin' o' youah time, an' time's the valuablest commodity what is, 'speciaily in this heah flourishin' an' hustlin' community. We're dealin' wiv a *he*poch, an' that's somethin' else again, as the Jew said when he saw the fire department comin'.

"I ain't agwine to waste youah time. I ain't agwine to waste nothin'. Ah's jes' agwine tell yo' all — ah's jes' agwine point out to yo' a half-a-dozen o' the leadin' circumstances what this heah pictchah as yo' all see dazzlin' yo' optics means. An' then ef yo' ain't the gratefullest niggahs what is, ah's agwine be the mos' mistakenest one.

"This heah's Moses. You all done heard o' Moses. He led the chillun o' Isr'el into a lan' 'at wuz flowin' wiv milk an' honey, after he'd showed 'em how to plunder the 'Gyptians. An' the 'Gyptian police what chased 'em to recover the di'mond brooches an' the watch-chains an' the stick-pins as they'd 'dopted 'fore they made their getaway was flummoxed by de good Lo'd an' drowned. Plum daid, ev'ry one of 'em, an' the chillun of Isr'el 'scaped.

"They wuz 'Gyptians, those police was. Mebbe the p'lice in this heah lan' o' bondage is all 'Gyptians too. I ain't looked 'em over 'nuff so's to be able to give yo' stric' information on that point. You'll jes' hev' to make use o' your discriminations an' discover that point for yo'selves. But that ain't the point izzac'ly as I wuz drivin' at.

"I'm agwine discuss wiv you tonight about Moses. He killed a 'Gyptian p'liceman — did it easy, 'cause the p'lice in those days didn't have no shootin' irons, an' Moses was that indignunt, what wiv the cop's fresh line o' talk an' one thing and another, that he smit him good an' hard. He nonplused that 'Gyptian, lef' his carcase lyin' there, an' beat it. The 'Gyptians sicked their blood-hounds after him, but the dogs in those days hadn't no more nose than jackrabbits, an' Moses giv' em the ha-ha, tendin' sheep so's to have somethin' in the envelope when pay-day come aroun'.

"He tended sheep for forty years out on a ranch somewheres, till the statute o' limitations run out an' his pictchah in the rogue's gallery wuz all faded — an' him so changed, what with the mean livin' on the ranch, and him growin' a beard, an' gettin' older, an' gettin' a new suit o' clo'es — til them 'Gyptians couldn't recognize him no more. Then he come back, 'cause the ranchin' weren't the fondest thing that he wuz of by no means. He was plum fed up with it. But he knew more'n he once did. There wasn't nothing you could tell him 'bout sheep.

"Well, he come back; an' he found the ol' house up on the hill, where he used to live, all fallin' to rack an' ruin' — win'ows busted in — no more taters in the tater-patch — rats runnin' roun' big as possums — place looked as if it wuz ha'nted; an' Moses looks aroun' an' sees a lot o' sheep on two laigs, workin' for the 'Gyptians. That started him off thinkin'.

"He went an' sat up on top o' the big Pyramid an' figured it all out, watchin' them Chillun of Isr'el workin' so hard for the 'Gyptians down below there; an' finally he came to a conclusion, them bein' things 'at any feller comes to when he makes his ol' bean work furious. An' Moses, he wuz plum furious all through.

He didn't want to go back an' live in that ole rack-an'-ruin shack of a place, full o' rats an' ha'nts an' no tater-patch nor anything. So he come to a conclusion, Moses did, an' him knowing what he did about sheep, he mighty soon got busy.

"Pretty soon he had all them Chillan o' Isr'el chippin' in to a fund, an' him keepin' the money, an' he says to 'em, 'What's the use o' you all makin' bricks without straw, when Ah knows a place where yo' kin all live easy without doin' a stroke o' work — an' all the honey an' milk yo' wants? Supposin' you-all down tools an' come along o' me,' says Moses. An' he shows 'em how to plunder the 'Gyptians first, him havin' no more feelin' o' pugnaciousness about p'licemen an' rather they'd do it for him. An' by-an'-by he has 'em comin' after him like sheep, all carryin' the brooches an' the gold earrings, an' they come to the Red Sea, an' he gets 'em over, an' the 'Gyptians is drowned, and they's all singin' an' lookin' forward. An' then he says to 'em, 'March!' says he, an' bes' foot forward, for you can't go back or the cops'll get yo', so there's nothin' else for it!' An' he keep 'em paradin' in the desert there for forty years.

"Walkin' the ties in Arizona weren't nothin' to it, for there weren't no ties nor yet no water-tanks. There weren't nothin', 'cep' jes desert, an' mebbe sage-brush, an' insec's, an' rattlers an' all kinds o' pizen snakes; an' when they did come on water it was all full of alkali so they could hardly drink it. And there weren't no bootleggers, chinks an' dagoes, sellin' 'em liquor to sweeten their stomachs. No, sir, them Chillan of Isr'el did their hikin' bone-dry; an' they plum wore out ole Moses wiv their complainin' an' all till he quit cold; an' he was all that fed up wiv 'em 'at he wouldn't have no funeral or nothin' but 'lowed he'd find himself a cave somewheres an' go an' die in that.

"But 'fore he died he took 'em up on Pisgah mountain, an' he says to 'em, 'Thar's y'r promis' lan'; go fight for it, yo' suckers!' An' he shows 'em the promis' lan' a mighty long ways off, all full o' folks they'd got to 'xterminate. 'Tweren't no big lan' neither. An' they couldn't see no honey 'less they worked to git, same as they did in Egyp'.

"Now, here's the point I'se comin' to. 'Tain't no little lan' we're aimin' for to git. We'se agwine git us a continent! When it comes to spoilin' 'Gyptians fust, we ain't magpies pickin' here an' there an' flittin' off, we's wholesalers! We're chesty. We're gwine he'p ourselves proper! They ain't nothin' we's agwine leave behind! We's agwine laff at ev'rybody, p'lice included! We're the really true an' only genuine P.O.P., which O stan' for omnibus an' means we's agwine take ev'rything, an' ride, not walk! The white folks in this lan' o' bondage is agwine sit still an' lock the p'lice inside the station house, so's we kin do it easy — jes' as ea-easy, as sayin' it!

"An' hike? Say; who are yo' kiddin'? We'se agwine ride the whole way! How come, you s'pose, that German fleet got sunk 'way over thar in Europe? Did you folks never hear nothin' 'bout dispensations? That wuz one o' them dispensations. We'se agwine lif' that fleet o' ships right up from th' bottom o' the North Sea, an' use 'em. How come? How's we agwine fer to do that? Eeasy! Jes' as ee-asy! We's agwine put tubes down under the sea an' blow those ole ships fuller o' hot air than a b'loon is o' laughin' gas, an' they'll come floatin' up to the top jes' like a lot o' ducks. Then we's agwine ride in 'em to Africa. That's what! Them's our omnibus.

"An' Africa? Oh boy! That ain't agwine turn out to be no delusion. We's all agwine be kings an' emp'rors when we gits there. Sure! Ev'ry lazy good-for-nothing black'll have an elephant to ride on, an' a big umbrella over his haid fer to keep the sun off'n him. There'll be eats enough to go 'round', an' no work to do but rollin' bones jes' to keep the money circulatin'. I ain't foolin' yo'! An' that's all gwine come about jes' 'cause o' this heah pictchah on a gole plate what white folks had fetched f'm Egyp!"

By that time he had to keep pausing between sentences to let the howls of laughter die before he could get another word in. The whole hall seemed to be rocking to and fro with mirth, and about the only two people in the place who weren't grinning from ear to ear were Allison and Mrs. Aintree. Allison could see no humor in it.

"Are they all dementit? Is the body makin' jokes?" he asked me behind uplifted hand.

And Mrs. Aintree could see nothing in it all but gross indignity inflicted on herself; nor could I blame her, especially as she floundered straight into the mud-puddle that I half-feared she would see in time. She went in with a splash — all two hundred pounds of her, and the noise of it gave birth to silence for about ten seconds.

"Stop!" she thundered, with both fists raised. "I'll not have another word of this! It's bad enough to have to sit here breathing this atmosphere without being insulted as well! I'll summon the police and have the hall cleared if I hear another word of sacrilege and treason!"

That turned the trick. The twenty or thirty "initiates" and "aspirants" who had seen their way clear to an easy living on the strength of her unusual doctrines, and who even yet had hopes, perhaps based on money unaccounted for, began to take Mrs. Aintree's part noisily. About fifty men got to their feet. Allison whipped the plate off the tray and stowed it in his satchel.

"Take that precious plate out of here!" bawled Mrs Aintree. "Take it away from their profane eyes!"

She was half-crazy with wounded vanity, but if she had been wholly mad she couldn't have made a worse break from her own stand-point, or a better one from mine.

"It's our gole plate! It's the P.O.P. gole plate!" somebody bellowed, and there began a rush for it as sudden as those gusts of wind that pick up a dust-whorl in the desert. It was exactly simultaneous with a rush by our own men, who reached the platform first, and just about sixty seconds in advance of an invasion by the Appleton police, who kicked the locked door open and wasted no time on preliminaries.

It's no use telling me there won't be fights in heaven. 'Twouldn't be heaven if that were so. Valhalla! We had to wade in! That crowd had had its laugh, and the laugh had kept it good-humored. But you'll find it safer to take a beef-bone from a wolfhound's jaws than to disillusion any swarm of men, colored or otherwise. The more they have laughed while the disillusioning went on, the swifter and the fiercer the reaction afterwards. Half those fellows realized that they had been made fools of from the first by Mrs. Aintree; others didn't know what to think, but decided to get the gold plate anyhow. The mob spirit accounts for the remainder. They all came on the run, some of them hurling chairs at us over the heads of the men in front.

It was one of the toughest jobs I ever faced, to get that gold plate and Mrs. Aintree out of Appleton town hall without injury to either. Sam was a wonder. He took the corner of the stage where the flight of steps led up from the floor, and none who saw him, or who met the calculated, swift ferocity of his attack, could ever more wonder why he wasn't wanted in the ring that time when they pocketed his forfeit money and railroaded him to jail instead. But there were too many of them, even for him; he got an ugly slash with a razor, and I had to leave Mrs. Aintree to the gang's protection and go to his aid. Since they had drawn razors I had no compunction about using chair-legs, and I bucked the swarm, brandishing one after the style of Samson when he slew those thousand Philistines with the jawbone of an ass. Only no ass' jaw, nor chair-leg could break a black man's skull, swat you never so emphatically.

The surprising part was that nobody pulled a gun on us. I had a pistol in my pocket, but didn't propose to use it against our own invited guests, except perhaps as an absolutely last recourse; and there was never a moment's real doubt of the outcome, with the police working their way toward the stage with the aid of night-sticks, going through their mob-drill like automatons, and turning suddenly at intervals to drive the rear of the mob out into the street. I dare say the whole business was over in five minutes, but it was a jewel of a fracas while it lasted; a jewel of a speech, too, that the chief of police, made from the front steps of the hall to the disgruntled remnants who remained to rub their heads and hear him.

"An' that's the last of this P.O.P. foolishness we'll have in this town, if yez have any sinse at all! Wan more word about it, an' I'll P.O.P. pop the lot of yez into the coop, an' what with foines an' jail-sintences ye'll wish ye'd never heard o' Moses, let alone seen his photograph! Get along home now, all of yez, an' step smart! And as for you, ma'am," he went on, turning on Mrs. Aintree, "I'm sorry to say I'm ashamed of ye! Ye ought to know better, for ye've lived here long enough. I knew y'r old dad an' your husband, or I'd say more. Good night, ma'am!"

He turned to me last, accepted a cigar, cocked it upward at the stars between his teeth, and grinned.

"We'll have peace here for a while," he said; "but — that's a wonderful pair o' fists ye have. Where the divvle did yez learn to use 'em?"

CHAPTER XI

"Man, the plate's gone!"

I WON'T GO SO FAR as to pretend that relations as between Mrs. Aintree and myself had been exactly cordial hitherto. They had not. But up to the point of that lodge meeting in Appleton we had been able to observe the amenities. We had presented to the world at large a reasonably amicable front. She detested and despised me, and while I did not overestimate her charms or her integrity I was rather sorry. for her, so we had managed to exist on the same Pullman car without exploding.

But to be made ridiculous was too much. I had committed the unforgivable offense. She hadn't a forgiving disposition at the best of times, but I had passed the Rubicon. She could no longer look at me without glaring; could not even see me without muttering; could not frame polite words in answer to the customary social salutations; and, on top of all that, she was imbecile enough to suppose that I wasn't alert for her vengeance.

It is only the secret enemy who is dangerous. The man or woman who makes faces at you, or defies you openly, is as easy as a rattler to contend with, for you have had notice. Her lust for revenge was as venomous as concentrated snake-juice, but she seemed to think herself possessed of a fairy-book cloak that rendered her hatred invisible.

A half-witted man would have realized the absurdity of her continuing another mile with us unless she were planning to upset my calculations.

When I canceled all arrangements next morning, and had to send sheaves of telegrams to shorten our itinerary and provide connections that would take us by the shortest route to Sparks,

Nevada, it must have been obvious to her that I had some other motive than to break up a P.O.P. lodge meeting. The P.O.P. was done for. Ridicule would finish it. Sparks, according to our reports, was the center where the movement had made less progress than anywhere else. But such people as Mrs. Aintree — and there are lots of them — are more fatalistic than the Moslem, and ascribe every unexpected move to a calculating Destiny.

She wanted to get to Sparks. I had changed all plans and decided to go to Sparks at once. Therefore, obviously, Destiny was playing her game, and in due course would deliver me to destruction, ably and vindictively assisted by herself. If you look around you'll find any number of people who habitually argue with themselves in some such way as that.

There began to be a sort of surreptitious glee observable in Mrs. Aintree's manner — a confident cocksureness blended with the hate, that would have forewarned an ostrich with its head stuck in the sand. She began to make an awful fuss over Sam, dressing his wound about three times as often as was necessary, and flattering him with honeyed words for having fought so nobly, as she expressed it, in defense of womanhood. Sam liked it. There never was a darky who didn't enjoy that kind of treatment. But when she gave him a telegram to send to Sparks he brought it to me immediately, and I let him keep it in his pocket for several days before dispatching it.

> *Antonio Vittori, Lakelock, California. All arrangements suddenly changed. Expect whole party at Sparks evening of thirteenth. Confident in your ability to devise and arrange solution. Count implicitly on me to carry out instructions, but would like them as soon as possible. Your pupil.*

FROM THE MORNING of our leaving Appleton until the thirteenth the railway people treated us to the loser's end of every gamble on connections. But we reached Sparks at last after an almost endless crawl across sage-brush desert that lies waiting for nothing but pumps and persistence to make a new Garden of Eden of it, and almost before the train rolled to a standstill half-an-hour after sunset our game began again in earnest. They cut our car off, and bunted it in the direction of the engine sheds — then trundled it back into a bit of rusty siding, where we could stay until Sparks became paradise, if we happened to feel that way about it and for all that anybody cared.

A fellow with a neck like raw beefsteak cross-rabbeted into furrows allowed that that would do, and turned his back to superintend the moonrise, and there we were — plus the local sheriff, two Italians — one of whom looked like a bootlegger and the other like Dante come to life again — and, marvel of all marvels, Terence Casey stepping forward out of semi-darkness, like a ghost in an old-time play!

"Yes, me boy, the —— it's me, an' a fine fool's errand ye've brought me on! Not send for me? I know ye didn't! Did ye write to Meldrum Strange, though? Did he sind five-an'-twenty telegrams to Washington, until they transferred me to this job, or did he not? And did I take the Overland, an' arrive here a day ahead av ye? I sure did. And of all the Devil's own places to have to waste time in, this is the Devil's choice, or my name's Moses, same as so many o' your friends! I'll introduce ye now to Mr. Arthur Brandon, county sheriff. Maybe ye don't know a man any longer when ye meet wan. This is him. Sheriff, this is Mr. Jeff Ramsden, elephant hunter and now lunatic at large; watch out f'r his grip, he's hefty!"

I looked straight into the eyes of the real West, the quiet, all-observing eyes that are used to vastness and afraid of nothing. He was as big as I am, standing with two fingers of his left hand hitched into his trousers pocket. His right came forward slowly for me to shake, and I liked him, warts, freckles, wrinkles, old gray flannel shirt, and all.

Forty years old, or a little more, with eyes of twenty-five; skin like leather; a ready smile; and a way of standing that pretended nothing, asserted nothing, except his own faith in the universe and his permission to all concerned to share it with him if they chose.

After the manner of his kind, he said nothing, conceding the first deal, or shot if you like, to the stranger.

"I'm watching those two whaps," I said. "It may be one or other of them has a message for someone in the car; if so, I want to know it."

Casey took that hint and drew apart to observe both car-ends from a point of vantage.

"I hope Casey has saved time by telling you most of the details of this business," I said, and he nodded.

"Casey and I had a talk last night, Mr. Ramsden. He doesn't seem to think much of your alarm."

"Are you willing to look into it with me?"

"You bet."

"Do you know a man named Antonio Vittori, a dago living just over the border at Lakelock?"

He nodded again. "Yes. Quiet man. Great studyer. Eyetalian, not a dago. They say he's all right."

"He's the man I'm after."

"Hell and damnation! Supposed to have murdered a colored man, isn't he? Do you figure that killing is always a crime, Mr. Ramsden?"

"I guess you and I would agree on most points, if we had time to discuss them," I answered. "Antonio Vittori is an Indian."

"Is that so?"

"I'm here to convince you. How far does your authority extend?"

"No further than the borders of this county. But there'll be no difficulty about getting the California bunch to help us out. You expect this Antonio Vittori here tonight?"

"Maybe. I suspect those two Italians. Are you sure he's not in Sparks this minute?"

"We can find out. Does he figure on killing a few more blacks? I notice you've brought along a lot of live-bait."

"We've a gold plate with us that he's nuts on. He killed that colored man to get the rest of the set — but the set's worth not much more to him than bullion without the one we've got, and he knows where it is. I believe he'll try to get it."

"New York State warrant in order?"

"Sure. Federal warrant, too, I believe; ask Casey about that."

"We'll take him and see what's in this. Well, Casey, what d'you make of it?"

"Ramsden's right. That whap with a face like Montezuma passed a letter to Mrs. Aintree. She's writing. He's on the platform waiting for an answer. The other whap beat it; I guess he's gone to tell someone that the letter was delivered."

"We'll soon see."

The sheriff turned to one of his assistant deputies, who was leaning against the side of the car, chewing tobacco, and listening alertly without asserting himself in any way.

"Shorty, I think it's up to you to follow that Italian who was here a minute ago. D'you know where he went?"

"Shore. I c'n see him now."

"See where he goes, and bring me word. I'll be here awhile yet."

The deputy walked off without comment, rolling himself a cigarette as he went, resembling by no means a salaried proponent of the written law. He looked more like a dry-goods clerk on his vacation, except for a certain measured litheness in his walk.

"Just a minute," said the sheriff. "There's one thing I can do right now."

He walked to the end of the car — the end that he had been watching across my shoulder — and reached it at the same moment that the Italian with the Dantesque face began coming down the steps.

"What are you doing?" he demanded. "Been stealing a ride? No? What have you got there?"

"All-righta, boss, I jus' taka letter, thass all."

"You — liar! You've been stealing!"

"No, boss! Honest to God! Strika me dead, I taka da letter."

"Cut the talk! Prove it!"

The Italian pulled an envelope out of his hip pocket. The sheriff snatched it out of his hand, glanced at it, showed it to me, and gave it back. It was addressed in a woman's hand in pencil to "Mr. A. V."

"All right. You get by this time."

The Italian hurried off.

"Have you got time to follow that man, Casey?" asked the sheriff, and Casey strolled away with both hands in his pockets.

"What did you figure on doing with this minstrel troupe you've brought along?" the sheriff asked me, and I countered with another question —

"Have you had any trouble in Sparks with a colored society called the P.O.P.?"

"Not what we'd call trouble in this part of the world. There's quite a number in the railway sheds. They hired an iron shack on the edge of town, and the talk in there went to their heads a bit. They got to pushing white men off the sidewalk. That was as far as it went. They don't use that shed no longer."

"Where do they meet now?" I asked.

"They don't. They were in that shed when we started to haul the uprights out from under it. There's a donkey-engine in the next lot, and we had a chain passed 'round the drum with a hook at the other end made fast to a couple of four-by-fours. They came out like black bats flitting out of Hell, and since then they been kind of superstitious about holding meetings. Why do you ask?"

"My plan was, supposing you agree, to turn my outfit loose

and let them get in touch with these P.O.P.'s. I hope to discover whether Antonio Vittori has been mixed up with the P.O.P. in this town. If so, we'll have another line on him, and —"

"Hell!" the sheriff interrupted. "Between you and Casey we've got lines enough. We'll pop over into California in my car, get a search warrant and a couple of deputies from over there, and look him up. If you've got the evidence, we'll fix him."

"Mrs. Aintree — she who wrote that note just now, and sent it by the Italian — is an accomplice of Vittori-Bhopal Gosh," I answered. "She has been sending him telegrams. He expects us here. He knows we've brought along a gold plate that he wants. He'll make a desperate attempt to get it; and he has almost certainly made arrangements for getting away directly afterwards. He's a damned clever rascal, and the last person in the world to find cooped up at home at a time like this."

"What's your idea anyway?" he answered, scratching the back of his head. "To set some kind of trap for him?"

"I'd hate to get Bhopal Gosh without the gold plates, and he may have hidden them."

"I'll give you any help I can."

"This colored gang of mine is hand-picked," I answered. "Let them circulate, and if they can find one of their race here in touch with Bhopal Gosh they'll send word that they're loyal P.O.P.s, and can steal that remaining plate and get it to him. He wants it badly enough to take a chance."

"H'm! Sounds rather like trapping a bear with sealing wax, but maybe I don't quite get the value of that plate — to him, I mean. As you say, if he's half-clever we'd hardly find him at home. All right, turn your gang loose. You'd better caution them. We've been cleaning up this town. Some of the boys might conclude to make a fresh start."

Our colored crew were interested in one subject only at the moment — supper, naturally. They were standing around us close enough to call attention to themselves, and no pack of hounds at a day's end could have looked more wistfully anxious.

Brice and Allison were packing up, methodical men both. They always arranged their compartment as if they expected visitors. Allison liked to have his spare shoes and slippers at the bottom of the bag, with the things on top laid neatly, so the business of tidying up took time. I wanted to call them out and introduce them, and had turned to do it, when something occurred to put that for the moment out of mind.

THERE CAME A HERD of colored men from the direction of the station platform, mostly in overalls, lurching along and laughing, obviously of one mind — a big, hefty-looking lot, and maybe forty of them. They approached our crew and began making the idiotic P.O.P. signs. In less than a minute there was a regular reunion taking place, with the sheriff and myself more or less in the midst of it.

"Things seem to be working out to suit you," said the sheriff.

I was looking about for Sam, he being the one who usually caught on to a notion quickest, and had just spotted him on the outside of the crowd, when Mrs. Aintree came hurrying heavily down the car steps and pushed her way toward me, shoving the darkies away to right and left as if they were so many nine-pins. She was in one of her towering passions — full of what she imagined was divine fire — so wrathy with self-righteousness that nothing but her own ideas and her own convenience had any weight as far as she was concerned.

"You wicked devil!" she began, marching right up to me. "I suppose you are planning to stage another sacrilegious farce! Who is this man?"

The men of the West have manners. The sheriff drew back until he was obscured in shadow, and began to take apparently intense interest in the conversation of the darkies.

"You will pay for all your doings!" Mrs. Aintree went on. "You think you're very smart. I know your thoughts; you think the money and the praise you'll get for this is recompense enough for all the harm you're doing! You're being well paid for it, and you simply ooze self- satisfaction! You're a disgusting sight, Mr. Ramsden, let me tell you that!"

"I'll give you permission to tell me that, if that's what's troubling you," I said.

"Troubling me? I am far from troubled!" she retorted. "I am simply trying to stop you before you destroy yourself with your own wickedness! You could do good if you chose, but you chose evil. The way of the transgressor is hard, Mr. Ramsden! You are laying up hell for yourself, and I would save you from it if I could!"

She meant every word of it, although, by holding my attention she was also forwarding an almost perfect piece of cunning. I believe she was obeying orders. She caught her breath for another outburst, but there came an interruption from the other end of the car — behind me in the dark.

"Help! Help!"

by Talbot Mundy   109

It was Allison's voice. I went to the rescue, but I'm a trifle slow at starting and the sheriff reached the steps ahead of me, swung himself up by the hand-rail, and was first into the car. I brought up short behind him. The doors of compartments A and B were fastened together, handle to handle, by a piece of stout wire twisted as if some one had used pliers for the purpose. It took time to unfasten them, for the wire was too thick to cut with an ordinary clasp knife, and all the while Allison kept wrenching at the door from the inside, taking up the slack and making our work more difficult. However, we got both doors open at last, and Allison came stumbling out with blood all over his face. Brice was lying unconscious on the sofa, bleeding too.

"Have ye got him?" Allison demanded.

"Got whom?" asked the sheriff.

"Ye mean ye've let him get away? Ye mean — My God! D'ye know what's happened? Did ye not see where he went? Are ye stricken daft? Oh this expedeetion! I knew from the verra first it was for-r-e-doomed!"

"Sit down and tell us," said the sheriff quietly, pushing him by the shoulders while I gave a hand to Brice, who seemed to be recovering consciousness.

"Man, the plate's gone! There cam' a dark-faced loon through yon door wi' a girt stick in his han', and wi'out sayin' one wor-r-d he struck at Brice an' me as if we were cattle an' he a flesher wi' a pole-ax! I held up ma han' to save Brice, for the fir-r-st blow was aimed at him, an' there — look! — there's where the blow landed on ma for-r-earm. Then he str-r-uck me in the face wi' his other fist, an' grabbed ma satchel. The strap broke! Then he struck Brice, who was up an' comin' for him. Then he struck me again, an' we were baith unconscious for I dinna ken how long — an' then I tried to get out an' ca' for help, an' the door was fastened! An' so the plate's gone — the only one we had, left — gone for good and a'! An' poor Brice dead — a good little man, a good little frien' was Brice; I'll not forgie' masel' "

"Your plans don't seem to he going quite so good, do they?" said the sheriff, eying me with a dry smile.

CHAPTER XII

"Feller, you were right just now!"

ALLISON, whose arm had really received the worst damage, insisted on having Brice taken to the hospital and mourned over him like a lost child. Maybe in that way the edge of his grief over the stolen plate was softened in some degree, which was as well, for only antiquarians can guess what pangs he suffered.

However, neither the sheriff nor Terence Casey showed more inclination than I did to take the theft for what diplomatists call a *fait accompli*. Casey and the sheriff's deputy returned together, and Casey was the first to get the hang of the situation.

"Those two whaps just walked about town," he said. "They knew they were being followed. They were decoys. I asked your deputy to lock up both av 'em up and they're in the coop now. There was nothing in the letter that wan av 'em carried. He knew it. It was blank paper."

"I get you," said the sheriff. "And these blacks, I guess, were sent down here to keep the other blacks from standing in the way inside the car."

"Then Mrs. Aintree came and bawled me out," said I, "to hold our attention while the trick was being worked. Bhopal Gosh sneaked up to the car from the far side, got a word in her ear, and — it all fits."

"Fits foine!" said Casey. "Just a minute."

Mrs. Aintree had shut herself into her compartment. Casey mounted the steps and rapped on her door. One or two of her meek minions tried to prevent him, but he kept on hammering until she called out "Come."

"You're under arrest — you and the lot av ye!" he informed

her through the open door. "Where's that letter ye received just now by the Dago?"

He came out swearing and laughing alternately, and showed us a handful of ashes.

"She burned it," he said, "and darn her, she broke up all the ashes in the spittoon! Ye can photograph whole ashes, but not broken wans!"

"Well, there's no place in our coop for a lady," said the sheriff. "We'll leave her in the car, and I'll set some one to keep watch. We've about one chance to take Vittori, or Gosh, or whatever his name is. Nevada's kind of big. If he once gets into the mountains, he'll be difficult to catch — have to send a posse after him and comb the woods. Home's the likeliest place where he'd cache the New York loot so's to have it ready for a getaway. He'll figure on beating back home — had his car parked somewheres close at hand. He'll aim to pick up the loot he cached at home and head for California. That's my guess. Any o' you good at guessing?"

"Anyone you can phone to in Lakelock?" I suggested.

"Wire's been down since yesterday. Trees are always falling across the wires. Not much of a job to fix, but devil's own time to get there, 'specially when the gangs are busy. If Gosh has a high-powered car and his nerve — and it looks as if he had — he's going to be hard to overtake. My car's ready."

Taking one thing with another, Bhopal Gosh had twenty minutes start of us, including five at a cafeteria where we threw some food into the car. Then we went like the fire chief to an "all turn out" alarm, with Casey and one deputy on the rear seat, and there was some " 'scuse it please" driving as we slipped out through the home-going cars of the railway hands and their families, most of them driven by women, and followed the trolley-line by way of Reno.

WE LEFT THE INTERURBAN car standing still, and whooped through Reno out on to the concrete pike without having killed anybody so far. Then the sheriff opened her out, and we really took a chance or two past Steamboat Springs, where the vapor from the cauldrons under ground hung like great ghosts over the landscapes. The only casualty as far as Carson was a cat that ought to have known better. It was a black cat, and Casey swore seriously.

"If it had been a white wan, now, that would have been the same as killing bad luck. But ye've killed the good luck, divvle take it!"

However, at Carson we got news, and knew, we were on the right trail. The sheriff drew up at a hotel where they once used to lay out the victims of shootings on the pool table, but now sell meals to ranchers' wives. There were half-a-dozen loungers in the bar busy bewailing the old days.

"Got anything to drink?" the sheriff asked.

"Nothing worth while," said the barkeep.

"Serve us some o' that. Anybody know Antonio Vittori — Lakelock way?"

"Sure." Two men knew him. "He passed through Carson in his car twenty minutes back."

"What sort of car? What make?"

"Didn't notice. — He's no auto thief. He don't need to steal nothin'."

"Big car or little one?"

" 'Tweren't a Ford — Hup — Overland — Reo — some such make — nothing a guy like him would help himself to. He's got money, I'm telling you."

"We'll get him! Come on. 'Night, you fellers. Did he go by Truckee or —"

"No, not Truckee. Up to the right — nearest way home I reckon."

We piled in, and the sheriff let her go again.

"That hill's going to slow him to a walk. Let's hope the gang's fixed the road for winter; no small car can clear the ridges without slowing for them, and if that's so we'll nab him inside Washoe County. Up she goes! Feel this brute purr — never knew a son-of-a-gun like this for eating hills."

The conversation grew disjointed, for the sheriff set his teeth and drove to suit Jehu son of Nimshi. The fellows behind were clinging to the seat, for the road-gang had put the ridges in; and every fifty or a hundred yards the car would kick like a cow pony just off grass.

The moon shone clearly enough to show the precipices on our left hand — sheer, gosh-grizzly things that fell away from under us for hundreds of feet with never a yard of clearance if another car should want to pass; and our lights showed hair-pin curves ahead such as made the reputations of the old stage-drivers. I kept my hair on by remembering that the sheriff would hardly use all that speed unless he knew the road intimately, but the little he said was scarcely reassuring.

"That's where the stage went over last June with eleven

passengers," he said once. "Weren't missed till next morning. Boys found 'em all dead but one, and he's still in hospital. This next curve we're coming to's a bitch. Hold tight! There, didn't I tell you. There'll be something happen there one o' these days; they ought to set that ridge about a rod this side of where they've got it. Tell those men behind to take a look at their guns. This Indian friend of yours may try conclusions. Darned good places hereabouts for a man to stand you up — that clump of trees ahead for instance. A few shots through your radiator. Sit tight here now!"

We swept around a curve with a yawning cliff six inches from the near wheels, and saw the whole of the finest valley in Nevada stretched in moonlight a couple of thousand feet below. Ahead, the road curved to the left at last, and we could see it snaking along, nearly milk-white, for a mile or two.

"There he is! See his lights? He's in trouble. No, he's off again. Changed a tire, I guess. Well, we've got him now."

"Unless he takes to the woods," I suggested.

"If the sucker does that we've got him sure!" said the sheriff. "Holding a line through these woods is quite a trick; we'd have him inside fifteen minutes. Sit tight, all, I'm going to step on her!"

IT CAME PRETTY CLOSE to being his last act in this world — close to being the curtain on the four of us. We were still mounting, but the grade was not so stiff and the speed indicator touched forty-five, then nearly fifty as we slid into the shadow of tall sugar-pines that loomed above the road on our right hand. Then, neatly as the picture of a screen slips off and gives place to another one, we swerved aside and went headlong over a steep bank. There was lots of time to think. It was like riding in an aeroplane, with all that moonlit valley smiling up at us.

The sheriff leaned forward and switched off the spark as the car took a sidewise tilt in mid-air, and we crashed into splintering tree-tops. The car remained up there, with one front wheel spinning on apparently forever in the calm moonlight, dumping cushions, tools, and us on to a ledge below that provided foothold for the friendly trees. I remember I thought it an awful shame that the trees should break our fall at such immense cost to themselves, but a fellow has strange thoughts sometimes in a crisis.

"That was a Hell of a way we came!" said the sheriff's voice from somewhere in the dark beside me. "Look at where we left the track — 'way back there! We coasted through the air forever, pretty near! My foot's busted. Anybody else hurt worth mentioning?"

"I'm killed!" said Casey's voice. "There's nothing holding me, but I can't move!"

The other man didn't answer, and I moved about trying to find him. When I stumbled on him he was breathing, and I lugged him and Casey to the sheriff's side, so that the two of us could feel them over, but you couldn't make sure in the dark.

"How did it happen?" I asked the sheriff.

"Hell. I caught sight of it too late. You remember we thought he'd changed a tire? All he'd done was fasten thick wire at an angle across the track, just high enough to ditch us; Smart, I'll say! Suppose you climb up and unhitch the wire before some one else comes along and gets hurt."

I climbed up. The wire was of the same thick gage that had been used to fasten the door-handles in the Pullman, and was wound three times around a tree-trunk, led across the road, and then made fast to a rock. If we had hit it straight we might have jumped or broken it, but the angle was such that you couldn't have hit it straight. Even going at slow speed it would have turned us outward over the side of the cliff, and it was nothing but the speed we were using that landed us among the trees instead of on the rocks this side of them. I let the wire down the cliff-side for a hold-fast, and clambered down to hoist those three men one at a time to the road. The sheriff came easiest; his ankle was very badly sprained, but he could help with two hands and the other foot. The other two had to be carried, and it took, I dare say, half-an-hour. Casey said he was in no pain, but felt numb all over, and the other fellow was obviously suffering from concussion.

"D'you suppose you'd be all right if I leave the three of you here?" I asked the sheriff.

"Sure. Going back for help? There'll be some one along in the early morning; we'll get picked up all right. Still, if you'd rather —"

"Will you be all right?" I asked him.

"Sure. What's eating you?"

"Then I'll go on. Give me directions how to reach that damned house. I'll go get him, or have a durned good try."

"Feller, you were right just now," the sheriff answered. "You and I would agree on most things. I guess I'll swear you in as deputy. Hold up your right hand; so, we'll call you sworn. Casey, you're witness. Remember: If you get him the California side of the line you've no jurisdiction. In that case plug him and do the arguing about it afterwards. If you catch him this side, plug him, and there won't be no argument. Have you got a good gun? Take mine."

"This one's an old friend."

"Now remember. He may go slow now, figuring on having ditched us good. I guess he saw our lights as we went over. I hate to lose that good car. Listen: Five miles up the road on the right-hand side there's a shack belonging to a man named Norcross. If his phone's working, call up every police station within a radius of thirty miles, and get a crowd started on the way to meet you at your man's house. Maybe old Norcross'll lend you a rig; but he's moody; you'll be taking a chance if you borrow his rig without asking."

"I'll take another chance or two," I said.

"Good boy. Now there's this: Bhopal Gosh may have his plans all laid for crossing Lake Tahoe by boat."

"How big's the lake?" I asked.

"Thirty miles by sixteen, and more than a mile deep where they've found bottom — coldest water anywhere — drowns you quick, and never gives up its dead. If he's got a boat, you try to get a car — take his maybe — and get around the lake to head him off. You'll be able to see his boat all the way across in this moonlight. Stop wherever there's a phone and keep the gangs wised up. Whatever you do don't follow him alone across the water. He'll spill you, and you won't stand a chance. Besides, a bit of a wind across that lake'll upset any but a stout craft, and the best are none too safe."

"How'll I find his house?"

"Can't mistake it. Follow this road about nine miles as straight as she'll take you. The side-tracks to the right all go to million-dollar huts where the Californians lead the simple life in Summertime. You keep straight on. His house is on the left, facing the lake. There's a garage in line with it big enough to hold four cars, and the house is a brown shingle affair with a of a big roof pitched steep like a hillside. It stands by a clump of sugar-pines, and whether he's got servants, or any one to help him put up a fight I can't say. Get to a phone, like I told you, and then watch the place and wait for help to reach you. Good luck! It's usually luckiest to shoot first; remember that!"

"Ye owld amachoor daytective! I'll bet ye the drinks ye'll never get him!" murmured Casey by way of farewell.

I VERY NEARLY OVERTOOK my man at the end of about two miles, for he really did have tire trouble and a hard job changing shoes. I came on the discarded shoe with a loaded revolver near it that he had let fall in the dust when he took his coat off, and saw his tail-light disappearing around a turn not three hundred yards ahead of me. He was not going fast. Either his engine was badly overheated, or else he was sure of having killed us, and overconfident. But no matter how fast you walk, a car going at only fifteen or twenty miles an hour is going to leave you pretty nearly standing still, and I didn't catch sight of his tail-light again.

In ordinary circumstances I would have reveled in that walk, instead of cursing every bend in the road that only showed another bend as soon as you rounded it — and that again another bend beyond. Some six or seven thousand feet above sea-level, the air was perfect and the scenery as wild as any man could wish. I even saw a bear lolloping across the road in front of me, and hove a rock at him out of sheer envy, because he might enjoy the solitude, whereas I must hurry on.

I made what I took to be Norcross's shack well within the hour, but there was nobody home. I made noise enough to wake anyone a mile away, and tried to break the door to get to the phone, but failed. However, there was a gray horse standing in the shed, and a spider-wheel rig that would just about hold together as long as the horse refrained from coughing. So I wrote a note on a leaf from my note-book, saying that the rig had been taken by a deputy sheriff and would be returned next morning, and drove away at a slow trot — the best that nag could offer. He had only three gaits anyhow; the second was a walk, and the third was to sit down on his rump between the shafts and think a while. So I let him trot, five miles an hour, or maybe six.

And try how I would I could find no telephone. All the places except one that I tried were unoccupied. In that place there was a Chinaman, who grinned and said, "No can do." He proved it, too, by letting me try the phone; it was as "dead" as Gulad the Abyssinian.

So I drove, and it began to feel lonely under those huge trees, with nothing to disturb the silence except an occasional windmoan and the clop-clop-clop of that disreputable horse.

As far as my experience goes it's untrue that a fellow reviews his whole career in a moment of time when death looks him straight in the face. But this I have found true — that when you're going forward to what you expect will be a crisis, all the circumstances that led up to it review themselves whether you will or not, until you are sick at heart from recognizing half-a-million mistakes you made and two or three opportunities you overlooked. After I left the Norcross shack I dare say I thought of thirty better ways to bring Bhopal Gosh to account.

Nevertheless, strangely enough, and unexpectedly enough, I didn't experience the slightest fear, until the old horse trotted around one last turn between sepulchral pines and cedars; and on my left hand, in a clearing, loomed the house that must be that of Bhopal Gosh, if the sheriff's description of it was correct.

Then fear struck me like a cold breath. There were no lights visible. There seemed to be nobody about. But I could hear an engine purring in the darkness by the front door, and the horse threw up his head and neighed.

CHAPTER XIII

"Lake Tahoe don't give up her dead."

I T OCCURRED TO ME to go at once and put that car out of commission. I might possibly need it for pursuit, but setting off one possible contingency against another it seemed wisest to dish the car. So I tied my borrowed Rosinante to a tree, walked up the drive, and tore out the wires leading through the dashboard to the switch. That was decidedly enough to delay Mr. Bhopal Gosh if he had not gone already.

However, as it turned out I made a mistake. I could have caught him handily by leaving that car purring away peacefully with its lights full on. But the minute I tore out that handful of wires the circular glow of white light cast by the lamps on the front of the house vanished simultaneously.

It didn't occur to me until then that Bhopal Gosh would not have left the house in darkness, with all that illumination on the outer wall, unless there was something to be gained by it.

It's not easy to puzzle out the other fellow's motives at a time when the least false move is likely to lose you the game. A crook thinks crookedly. If you've spent your waking moments for thirty or forty years endeavoring to think straight you're out of harmony with a villain's reasoning.

All that I accomplished by extinguishing the light was to give Bhopal Gosh notice that someone was close on his trail. That glare on the house wall had been visible from the lake shore, a quarter of a mile away, and I now saw somebody come carrying a lantern from the lake toward the house. He was coming in a hurry — didn't notice that the lights had gone out until he nearly reached the road, still well out of pistol range, perhaps two hundred yards from where I waited. Then he saw my gray horse, for the moon had dispersed the shadow in which I left him standing.

I tried to figure out what I would do if the positions were reversed, but gave it up. I didn't know why he was returning to the house. I remembered one of Terence Casey's sayings that "crooks, me boy, always overlook something, for that's the natur' of a crook. Ye catch 'em because they blow their noses on a dead man's handkerchief, or some such idiotic stunt as that."

That didn't help much. Bhopal Gosh wasn't blowing his nose. In fact, I couldn't see him, I could only see the lantern. I watched the lantern steadily for several minutes, until it dawned on me that it was hanging from a twig and its owner had gone elsewhere.

The odds were now that he was hunting me. As he knew the ground and I didn't those odds were a hundred to one in his favor. I elected to stay where I was for the moment, between the car and the front door, listening for a footfall that would give me a hint of his whereabouts. I heard two sounds — first, the pop from the exhaust of a motor-boat engine down by the lake shore. But he hadn't had time to reach the boat. I decided that the boat was moored, with its engine running, ready to get under way the moment its owner should come.

The next sound came from the direction of my rig. I heard the shafts fall to the ground — a smart slap as somebody hit the horse — and then the click of hooves as the beast started off homeward at an easy trot. It was like a game of Freeze-out — funny, if I'd been in a mood to laugh. I had put out of action a car that he possibly didn't want, and had demobilized myself as far as possible pursuit went; he had discovered that not more than two men were on his trail; for that rig would have broken down under the weight of more than two. And he had cut off my retreat.

What puzzled me most was, why he didn't make straight for the motor-boat. I heard his heavy footsteps over to my right behind a row of trees, and he was walking as if he weighed a ton, breaking twigs and crashing through the undergrowth like an elephant at feeding-time. I elected not to walk into that trap. Time was all in my favor.

IF I had been sure that he hadn't another car waiting at the rear of the house I would have headed for the boat at once and put that out of commission; but it was possible he was calculating on my doing just that, and did have a car in reserve; so I waited, not so much reasoning really as acting from intuition and habit developed in hunting days. It was that refusal to come out in the open and be seen that forced his hand. He had to try to unmask my batteries somehow, and took a rather silly way of doing it.

He began to scream like a beast in agony, pausing to wait for a reply and then screaming louder. As that had no result he yelled in English that he was caught by the leg in a bear-trap. If it was true I was glad to hear it; he might stay in the trap. I was certainly not going to be such a fool as to go and investigate; and what was more, he had done me the favor of demonstrating that he was all alone, for obviously any one within hail would have gone to his assistance; but nobody did go. He left off yelling after a few minutes, as a man at all prone to yelling would hardly do with his leg caught in the iron jaws of a bear-trap. Those things hurt.

Continuing to puzzle away at the problem I decided that he had gone down to the motor-boat to get the engine started, and had then come back to the house for his treasure. Perhaps there had been some doubt in his mind whether he could start the engine, and he had preferred to make sure before committing himself to that means of escape. If those heavy gold plates were in the house yet it was hardly likely that both he and they would escape me before morning.

But he had grown suspiciously quiet again, and I listened intently, wishing that contact with cities and railroads hadn't dulled my hunting ear. I could hear the motor-boat popping away steadily, but not one sound from Bhopal Gosh. The lantern, swaying gently on its twig, still burned brightly where he had left it.

His next move took me utterly by surprise. The porch light was switched on suddenly from inside the house, and I stood exposed between the door and the car at point-blank pistol range. I ducked around behind the car, astonished that I wasn't fired at; and, from that position, peering under the top, I caught sight of his face looking through a window to the right of the front door. I pulled the wrong pistol from my pocket — his that I had picked up in the road beside the abandoned tire — took a snap shot at him, and missed. But he didn't shoot back. It dawned on me that I had his only firearm! True to Terence Casey's dictum, the arch-crook had overlooked one simple, necessary point!

That settled it. I smashed in the window with the pistol-butt, and scrambled in, cutting my hand, but as luck would have it not badly enough to make it useless. The door at the end of that room slammed in my face, and I heard the key turn on the outside, but I took a heavy chair and swung it ax-fashion, breaking the door down in less than a minute. That let me through into the hall. He had switched the light off, and was doing something in a devil of a hurry, for I could hear his heavy breathing not far off. Then I caught the metallic hum of a safe opening, and the rattle of the handle of the inner, sheet-iron door as he fumbled with it in the dark. By the sound I judged he was at the end of the hall, so I fired the same pistol I had used before to try and catch sight of him by the flash — or hit him if I happened to be lucky.

What I did see was the wall-button that controlled the electric current. I heard another door slam, and by the time I had switched the light on Bhopal Gosh was gone; but he had not removed the plunder, although he did get away with the key to the inner door of the safe.

The safe stood under the main stairway, and was an inexpensive affair with a combination lock on the outer door, which he had left unfastened in his hurry. I dare say I could have forced that inner door without much trouble if given time, but it seemed wiser in the circumstances to leave the treasure in there and return when I had reckoned with the man. He wasn't likely to be doing nothing while I fooled with the safe.

So I went back for another chair and smashed the door on the right-hand side of the safe that he had disappeared through. It was a good, heavy office chair with an iron revolving screw in it and iron-braced legs, so the door went down in short order; but at that I wasn't in time. There was a cellar below-stairs piled high with old, dry cord-wood, and as the door crashed outward a stinging cloud of white smoke met me with the crackling of blazing bark and splinters.

I charged through, with the idea of catching him before he could take advantage of the smoke to give me the slip altogether. I was holding his pistol in my right hand, having shoved it in my hip pocket while I used the chair for a battering-ram, making two pistols in one pocket, and as I rushed through I grabbed the first one that my fingers closed on. Bhopal Gosh was waiting for me just inside the door, and seized me by both arms from behind.

IT NEEDED no expert in intuition to guess what his game was then. He meant to hurl me down into the blaze below, and return for the contents of the safe. And it was a new experience to discover myself almost helpless in the arms of a stronger man. All up and down the world I have only met three amateurs who could beat me with their fists or on the mat, and they had to work for their laurels. But this fellow twisted the revolver out of my right hand with the ease of a gorilla, and flung it down the cellar stairs into the galloping holocaust below us.

"Yah-ah-ah!" he laughed.

But it was an expensive little joke, for as he let go my right hand to hurl the weapon away I swung sharp round to face him and crashed my fist into his mouth, cutting it a second time on his magnificent teeth, but giving him far the worst of the exchange. However, he had me by the wrist again before I could reach for my own revolver, and luckily — so swift he was — before he even guessed that that was my intention!

The heat was already terrific. Once or twice when a draft caught them the flames licked over the top of the cellar stairs, and he started to force me backward toward that hell, grinning in my face malevolently as he stepped forward like a great fat dancing-master — only it was muscle that made him bulk so big. It was the first time I ever felt really helpless in the grasp of a stronger man, and after the first strain that warned me of his enormous power I wasted no more energy on trying that issue with him.

I relaxed my muscles suddenly. By the light that roared behind me I could see the triumphant malice in his face; but he was in no hurry; he was enjoying the foretaste of victory — grinning like a great ape. You could see bow he had been so easily mistaken for Italian by men who were not suspicious of an alias, yet his face grew more Mongolian as you examined it. And he took care that I should examine it, thrusting it close to mine in order to peer into my eyes.

"You feel the fire behind?" he sneered. The brute wasn't even out of breath.

"You are going down into it backwards! But we will wait just a minute or two and let the flames take hold, because there is a door leading from that cellar to the garden, and you seem to have a gift for breaking doors!"

He thrust his great, dark face still closer to mine, so that his enormous shoulders rose higher than his neck. I guessed him at fifty inches around the chest, with every other detail in proportion, but he may have been bigger than that.

"I am curious about you!" he went on. "You are not of the police. Are you one of those poor fools who discovered a treasure that they could not keep? You are too unwise for Providence — I suppose you would call it Providence? — to leave it in your hands!

You would not know how to use it. I do. I shall use it! I shall leave you roasting here, and take it away with me! You're not talkative! It's your last chance to talk, you know, until you come into the world reincarnated as a beetle or a rat! You don't like the prospect of being burned to death? It terrifies you? Too bad! You would prefer the butt of Malmsey wine selected by the Duke of Clarence?"

Even the least astute of us become one horse philosophers as we grow older. When any man starts boasting in my face I take courage. Boasting is the inevitable prelude of disaster. I'm convinced of that, and an ounce of conviction is worth a ton of anybody's argument. I knew that minute that he might hurl me down into the fire, but if so he was coming with me, and I guessed I could face those flames as well as he could.

Maybe he read the determination in my face. He started there and then to force me backward, and I tried to throw him with a trick of the heel. He saved himself from that, but lost his balance; and I got my left fist free, gaining a good two yards away from the flames and sending my left home three times, once into his wind and twice into the region of his jaw. He had to let go my right wrist to protect himself, and I got my right home into his left eye before he closed.

Then, gripping like a bear, he began to force me backward once more, lifting me as my ribs cracked under his pressure. He had me under the arms, which left both fists free; and I rained blows on his mouth and eyes that would have taken some of the fight out of a Spanish bull. I guess I blinded him for the moment. I could feel the sickening scorch of the flames behind me as the floor-beams and door-posts caught; but I caught him by the neck and swung clear, and if I hadn't been in too much of a hurry he would have gone down into the cellar instead of me, for I drove for the region of his ear with my right fist, and the blow went wild.

Then I thought of my own revolver in my right hip-pocket, and he thought of all outdoors. The smoke and flame were blinding; the back of my jacket was smoldering, and I think his coat was too. At any rate, with his eyes half-shut and with the floor-beams beginning to crack under our combined weight, he lowered his head and charged me like a bull. Instead of meeting him with my knee, as I should have done, I stepped aside, took a shot at him, and missed! Missed him at fifteen inches! So much for smoke in the face.

We both went out of the house like rabbits running from a

grass fire, he straight by way of that nodding lantern for the motor-boat, and I after him, with the flames behind us lighting up all the windows now as they caught the draft from the open front door. It was only a matter of seconds before the whole house was a raging furnace.

I was out of breath, for he had crushed my ribs in badly, and on top of that I had swallowed a lungful of acrid smoke. What was worse, I am built rather for heavy work than running races; and for a man of his prodigious weight and strength he was fleet-footed. But he ran with his hands to his eyes. I had done him harm enough to equalize the odds.

Moreover, he wasted energy. His shortest course to the motor-boat was not by way of the lantern. In order to take the lantern en route he had to cover two sides of a broad-based triangle, giving him at least an extra hundred yards to run. Yet he did that, and I took the shorter route to cut him off, wondering what strange frenzy possessed him and supposing that his eyes might be so badly hurt that he was running half-blindly for whatever he could see.

Yet he didn't pick up the lantern. He paused there for half-a-second, tugging at something else that shook the lantern to the ground as it came loose from the tree, and carried whatever it was away with him. He was still in the lead by a dozen yards, and I tried a shot as I ran, with no result except apparently to increase his speed; and of course I had to slow down for a second in order to take aim, which gave him a few more yards of advantage.

I had now four shots left, and no spare cartridges. On the other hand, in spite of the pace, I was beginning to feel better as the smoke got pumped out of my lungs. Moreover, the fire by now was enough to alarm the countryside; they would turn out to save the forest trees if nothing else, and it was likely I would have help any minute.

Yet he was gaining on me — careering like a hippopotamus for his own element, covering an ell to my yard as he crashed through and over everything. I never saw any man take such enormous strides as he did, and all the way with his hands before his face, as if I had done his eyes real damage.

He was easily fifty yards ahead when he reached the water's edge and hesitated before jumping to the beach below. In that uncertain moonlight, and with my hand no doubt trembling from the run, it seemed like a fool's chance to take another shot; yet I took it — stopped dead, aimed carefully, and fired. I hit him. He dropped something that was hanging from his arm, clapped his hand to his side, and toppled sidewise over the bank.

I did that last fifty yards in record time — my record at all events. I figured on jumping on him from the top of the bank and finishing the business. But when I reached the bank he was clambering off a short plank pier into the boat and snatching feverishly at the lines to cast loose. He had made the boat fast in two places, which was in my favor; but he got both lines free; and the instant he had thrown the clutch into gear and opened up the gas, he crouched below the boat's side.

I remembered then that there is such a thing under heaven as horse sense. I could have easily wasted my three remaining shots in an effort to plug him but the boat was a considerably larger target. I fired all three deliberately, plunk into the boat, and one of them damaged the engine.

It doesn't take much to stop one of those single-cylinder affairs. I hadn't done much harm to the engine, for he got it going again in less than a minute; but during that minute the water must have made headway through two bullet-holes, and by the time he began to pay attention to it the water was swishing all over the bottom. What with the state of his eyes and the darkness he couldn't find the trouble. For a minute or two after that he seemed to be lifting off the seat-covers and looking for a pump, but there was none, for he began bailing with a small tin can. Then the engine gave a final cough and quit for good.

I lit a cigar. I'm willing to take oath that if there had been a boat within reach I would have put off and tried to save him for the hangman. But there wasn't any boat. I dare say he had taken care there shouldn't be. And as for swimming — he might swim in that nearly ice-cold water if so minded; I tested it with my hand and knew that I for one couldn't stay afloat in it for two minutes.

One of my bullets must have done much more than bore a hole in the hull, for he could have bailed against two or even against three bullet-holes. But though he worked like fury the water gained on him, and I could see the hull submerging inch by inch.

He lost his courage in the end completely. The chill of that rising water around his legs gave him too definite a foretaste of what was coming. He began to scream for help and to call on some Deity I never heard of. I tore two planks off the pier and hurled them as far as I could out into the lake, but he was a quarter of a mile away, and I doubt even if he saw me throw them. He could never have reached them anyhow.

He went down screaming, and the cold calm water closed over him with a ring of ripples that danced in the moonlight until the last, ever-widening circle nearly reached the shore. Then I turned to examine whatever it was that he had dropped when my bullet touched him, and clambering up the bank discovered nothing less than Allison's leather satchel.

YOU'LL BE RIGHT if you suppose that I unbuckled the flap with trembling fingers. Maybe I shouted — I don't know — when I discovered the gold plate safe inside. But it was badly damaged. My bullet had struck it near one corner, ploughed through the soft gold for several inches, itself expanding as it went, and finally had gone clear through to expand its last momentum on the ribs of Bhopal Gosh. The plate had been further damaged when he dropped it, for it was bent out of shape, and I think he must have stepped on it, because a good deal of the scripture was obliterated. Nevertheless, it was the plate, and I had at least something to return to poor old Allison.

There was no more chance of recovering the other plates than of gleaning snow on the plains in midsummer. We had left the outer safe-door open, and the whole house was a roaring furnace. It might be possible, when the ashes should cool off, to recover a shapeless mass of nearly pure gold; but it was far more likely that the safe had tilted forward as the beams gave way underneath it and the stuff as it melted had run out and got lost so thoroughly that its recovery would cost more than the game was worth.

I tried to get some of the fellows who came racing to the fire to help find a boat and look for Bhopal Gosh, hut when I told them sufficient of the circumstances they laughed at the idea.

"Never dragged a corpse out o' that lake yet, unless in the shallows inshore. The cold sets them solid. The body don't form no gas, and they stay down there a mile deep. No; Lake Tahoe don't give up her dead, and never will till Judgment Day."

So I borrowed a big car instead, and got two of them to come back along the road and help me with the sheriff, Terence Casey, and the deputy. Less than an hour later, as we drove dead-slow around a bend, I heard the sheriff's voice —

"I notice you got your man!" he called out.

Now I don't know how he knew that, nor would he tell me how he knew; but he swore that he knew it from the moment that our headlights came in sight around the corner.

I asked the deputy about it, who was not much the worse for his experience by that time, and he laughed.

"Shore he knew!" he answered. "He weren't guessing. He told us two that you'd got your man 'fore ever he spoke to you at all. Didn't he, Casey?"

"He did that," said Casey. "It all comes o' running over that black cat. Any man in his senses knew that somebody was going to get the gate tonight. Well, Lord be praised it wasn't me! I'm due for me pension. Hey, steady! Lift me easy — easy, you! I'm not the inimy, Ramsden! Ye're after pulling me to bits!"

SO IF you should have the good luck to visit London one of these days, and should have the sound horse sense and taste to pass a portion of your time in the British Museum, turn first into the Egyptian Gallery. And if you see there in a glass case by itself a battered gold plate with a great trough plowed across it so as to obliterate the head and shoulders of what was once the portrait of a man, you'll understand how it came there. They have marked it, "Very ancient; probably period of Israelitish occupation; mostly illegible; purpose unknown." For they are cautious men who conduct that institution.

But there's a middle-aged Scotsman attached with no very definite duties to that department. They say he is rather a mental wreck, and has been more or less pensioned in that way. He'll tell you the whole story of that gold plate, and better by far than I have done. But better not mention my name to him, for he vows, and will vow to his dying day, that I know quite well where the rest of the plates are, and that I mean to unbury them some day and offer them for sale when I suppose the game is safe.

"But just ye watch!" he'll tell you, in case you should mention me. "I'll balk him! I'll expose the chiel! I'll bring him to his downfall yet!"

Brice, on the other hand, is still digging for antiquities in Egypt; and he and I are great friends.

And if you should happen to meet Terence Casey — he'll be guarding a President, or tracking down a forger, or some such child's play — you might remember me to him; and if he says to you, as he surely will the minute that you mention me —

"My friend Ramsden is a well-meanin' man, I'll have ye know, and a good man of his inches. He knows a of a lot about ilyphints, and if he had his rights he'd be with a circus, or curatin' at the Bronx Park Zoo. But he's gone into the amachoor daytective business, and that's not a fit subjec' for conversation — not with prohibition running wild!"

If he says that to you, as he will, you might remind him that he owes me a round of drinks — a point that he unaccountably forgot when he came out of hospital. And you might add, that as good drinks are hard to come by these days, I'd be grateful if he'd come across.

And as for what became of Mrs. Aintree, and of the foreign entanglements of the P.O.P., most of which we had to straighten out before our job was done, let me remind you all once more of those Indian story-tellers, who invariably pause and pass the hat when it would seem that their audience has had its money's worth.

"Kull khadami tilzam. Allah yihfazak;" and may all your ways be peace!

THE END

www.ingramcontent.com/pod-product-compliance
Lightning Source LLC
Chambersburg PA
CBHW020145180626
46810CB00004B/1744